Praise for Shane Peacock and
THE BOY SHERLOCK HOLMES SERIES

"The first intriguing volume in an ambitious new series. . . . A shadowy, vividly described London. . . . Creative references to Doyle's characters abound . . . and Sherlock himself is cleverly interpreted. . . . Plenty of readers will like the smart, young detective they find here, and find themselves irresistibly drawn into his thrilling adventures."

– Starred review and named one of the
Top Ten Crime Fiction for Youth from *Booklist*

"The details of the plot are plausible, the pacing well timed, and the historical setting vividly depicted . . . The titular crow comes fascinatingly into play. . . . On balance, the characters enrich the book and help give Holmes's storied abilities credence."

– Starred review, *School Library Journal*

"In *Eye of the Crow*, Shane Peacock has created . . . a thrilling, impeccably paced murder mystery. Peacock reveals the budding detective's very real fears and insecurities, providing just enough detail about the young Sherlock's methods to make him an entirely believable teenage precursor to the master detective. Peacock also neatly creates a sense of the bustle of Victorian London, making the squalid grunginess of the East End almost waft off the pages."

– Starred review and chosen as one of the
Books of the Year 2007 from *Quill & Quire*

"The fast-paced adventure is a treat . . . those who enjoy the original Holmes stories will take pleasure in the . . . premonitions of things to come and the nature of this 'prequel.'"

– *The Globe and Mail*

Also by Shane Peacock

Eye of the Crow
Death in the Air
Vanishing Girl
The Secret Fiend
The Dragon Turn
Becoming Holmes
The Dark Missions of Edgar Brim

The Boy Sherlock Holmes  His First Case

EYE *of the* CROW

SHANE PEACOCK

tundra

First paperback edition published by Tundra Books, 2009
Text copyright © 2007 by Shane Peacock

Published in Canada by Tundra Books, an imprint of Penguin Random
House Canada Young Readers, a Penguin Random House Company

Published in the United States by Tundra Books of Northern New York,
an imprint of Penguin Random House Canada Young Readers, a Penguin
Random House Company

Library of Congress Control Number: 2006940128

Library and Archives Canada Cataloguing in Publication

Peacock, Shane
Eye of the crow : his first case / Shane Peacock.
(The boy Sherlock Holmes)
ISBN 978-0-88776-919-1

1. Holmes, Sherlock (Fictitious character)–Juvenile fiction.
I. Title. II. Series: Peacock, Shane. Boy Sherlock Holmes.

PS8581.E234E94 2009   JC813'.54   C2008-903713-8

Design by Jennifer Lum & Derek Mah

The author wishes to thank Patrick Mannix and Motco Enterprises Ltd.,
U.K., ref: www.motco.com, for the use of their Edward Stanford's Library
Map of London and its suburbs, 1862.

Printed and bound in USA

www.penguinrandomhouse.ca

8 9 10 11   21 20 19 18 17

Penguin
Random House
TUNDRA BOOKS

To my mother,
Susan Jane,
who gave me a writer's soul.

"During my long and intimate acquaintance with Mr. Sherlock Holmes I had never heard him refer to his relations, and hardly ever to his own early life . . . I had come to believe that he was an orphan with no relatives living; . . . "
     – Dr. Watson in *The Greek Interpreter*

CONTENTS

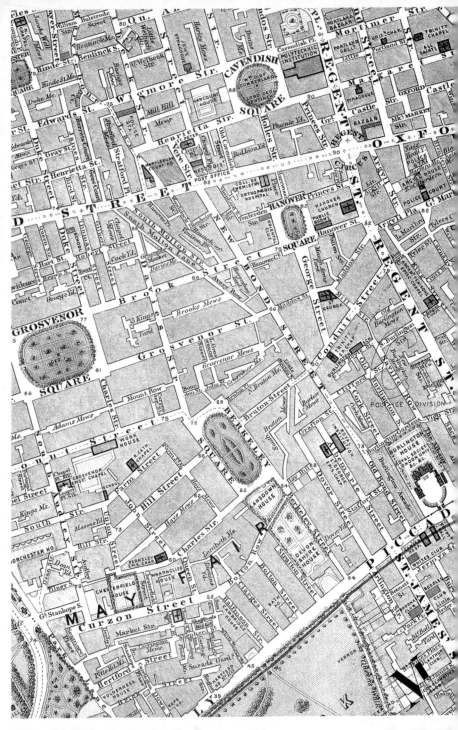

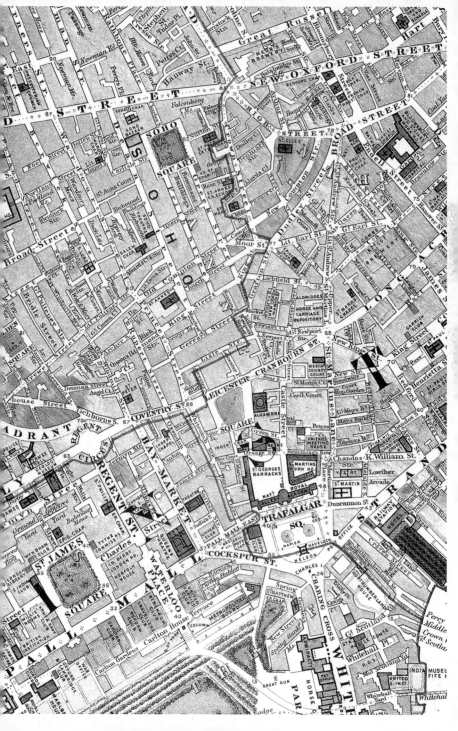

PREFACE

Murder came in darkness. It came in Whitechapel, far from the gaslights of the main
streets, to the east where the Jews were,
where the poor starved, where the invisible
people of the world's greatest city lived like animals. It came in
an instant, in a stab of brutality, unjust and violent.

Hours later, south of the River Thames in Southwark,
above a shabby shop in a narrow row near a slum, a boy reluctantly rose to meet another morning. Justice lived far from here
too. But today would mark the beginning of a reckoning: for
him, for that death, and for many crimes that would follow.

No one had seen the Whitechapel murder.

But in that night black eyes were watching.

And in this morning . . . the Master was awakening.

THE UNUSUAL BOY

As the sun climbs, its rays spread light through the lifting yellow fog, filtering down upon a brown, flowing mass of people: on top hats and bonnets, heavy clothes and boots swarming on bridges and along cobblestone streets. Hooves strike the pavement, clip-clopping over the rumbling iron wheels, the drone of the crowds, and hawkers' cries. The smell of horses, of refuse, of coal and gas, hangs in the air. Nearly everyone has somewhere to go on this late spring morning in the year of Our Lord, 1867.

Among those moving over the dirty river from the south, is a tall, thin youth with skin the pallor of the pale margins in *The Times* of London. He is thirteen years old and should be in school. From a distance he appears elegant in his black frock coat and necktie with waistcoat and polished boots. Up close, he looks frayed. He seems sad, but his gray eyes are alert.

His name is Sherlock Holmes.

Last night's crime in Whitechapel, one of many in London, though perhaps its most vicious, will change his life. In moments it will introduce itself to him. Within days it will envelop him.

He comes to these loud, bustling streets to get away from his problems, to look for excitement, and to see the rich and famous, to wonder what makes them successful and appreciated. He has a nose for the scent of thrilling and desperate things, and all around these teeming arteries, he finds them.

He gets here by the same route every day. At first he heads south from the family's first-floor flat over the old hatter's shop in grimy Southwark, and walks in the direction of his school. But when he is out of sight he always veers west, and then sneaks north and crosses the river with the crowds at Blackfriars Bridge, for the glorious center of the city.

Londoners move past him in waves, each with a story. They all fascinate him.

Sherlock Holmes is an observing machine; has been that way almost since birth. He can size up a man or a woman in an instant. He can tell where someone is from, what another does to make his living. In fact, he is known for it on his little street. If something is missing – a boot or an apron or a crusty doorstep of bread – he can look into faces, examine trousers, find telltale clues, and track the culprit, large or small.

This man walking toward him has been in the army, you can tell by his bearing. He's pulled the trigger of his rifle with the calloused index finger of his right hand. He's served in India – notice the Hindu symbol on his left cuff link, like one the boy has seen in a book.

He walks on. A woman with a bonnet pulled down on her head and a shawl gripped around her shoulders brushes against him as she passes.

"Watch your step, you," she grumbles, glaring at him.

An easy one, thinks the boy. *She has recently lost in love, notice the stains around her eyes, the tight anger in her mouth, and the chocolate hidden in her hand. She is within a year of thirty, gaining a little weight, a resident of the Sussex country-side where its unique brown clay has marked the insteps of both her black boots.*

The boy feels like he needs to know everything. He needs advantages in a life that has given him few. A teacher at his school once told him he was brilliant. He'd scoffed at that. "Brilliant at what?" he had muttered to himself. "At being in the wrong life at the wrong time?"

On Fleet Street, he reaches into a cast-iron dustbin and pulls out a handful of newspapers. *The Times* . . . toss it back. *The Daily Telegraph* . . . toss it back. *The Illustrated Police News* . . . ah, yes. Now there is a newspaper! Every sensation that London can create brought to life in big black-and-white pictures. He reads such scandal sheets every day, but this one, with a riveting tale of bloody violence and injustice, will reveal to him his destiny. He tucks it into his coat.

At Trafalgar Square he looks up to find the crows. There are often a few in a row on the edge of Morley's Hotel near majestic Northumberland House on the southeast side, a league from the fat pigeons and the crowds near the fountains. It makes him smile. One of the most prestigious hotels in all of London, crowned with crows. They're Sherlock's kind of birds.

He weaves through traffic and crosses the square to a spot on the stone steps of the National Art Gallery. The black birds move too. Sometimes, he thinks that crows follow him. A couple swoop down and settle nearby.

"Good morning, you two. Let's see what's in the news."

He unfolds the paper. The front page shouts at him.

MURDER!

Under the headline is a lurid drawing of a beautiful young woman lying on a London street, soaked in a pool of blood.

The crows shriek and fly off. Sherlock reads on.

It had happened east of the old part of the city in the dead of night. No one had seen it or even heard a scream. A long, sharp knife had been used.

Sherlock turns the page. He devours the story: a lady of mysterious social status, no name revealed, no known enemies. He realizes with a start that she looks like his mother.

The boy hears people talking as they walk by.

"That poor woman."

"Must have been a street person, a foreigner."

"There's that dreadful boy sitting there again. I wish he'd move on."

"Were they crows? That's not a good sign."

"Dodgers they are. Nothing but gypsies, I say. Here they come! I'll call the constables."

Sherlock glances up. It's the Trafalgar Square Irregulars. He can almost smell them.

"Master Sherlock Holmes, I perceive," says a dark-haired, tough-looking boy at the head of a dirty gang who are smaller copies of their leader. He is dressed in a worn-out long black coat with tails, a dark stovepipe hat is perched at an angle on his head, and he carries a crude walking stick in his hand. "I think you're sitting in our spot."

They've never sat here, nor will they today. They gather around and loom over him.

"My dear Malefactor . . . " replies Sherlock. He waves at the Irregulars, " . . . and friends."

"At least I have some."

"Quite."

"Move! Or we'll beat on you again."

"'alf-breed Jew-boy!" snarls a nasty one named Grimsby, of whom Holmes is always wary. His yellow, sharp-pointed teeth look like a ferret's, ready to bite.

Sherlock gets to his feet and straightens his third-hand clothes. He hates Malefactor; hates him with the deepest admiration.

"Seen this?" he asks, holding up *The Illustrated Police News*.

"Slit 'er from stem to gudgeon, 'e did! Right steady job!" shouts Grimsby.

The boys laugh.

"It isn't funny," says Malefactor, silencing them. "It isn't right."

"What's the word?" asks Holmes, aware that the young swell mobsman and his gang know every rumor that creeps through the alleys of London.

"For the streets to know . . . and keep to themselves," says Malefactor. "I don't like the –"

"I know," sighs Sherlock, "I know . . . you don't like the look of me."

There is something vaguely similar about the two boys, though the gang leader is a little older and speaks with a barely detectable Irish lilt. It goes beyond their dark looks. It is in their way of expressing themselves and the careful manner they dress in their tattered clothes. They both know it, but Malefactor doesn't like it.

"You'll never be an Irregular. Not you, Sherlock Holmes."

"And yet, I'm as irregular as I can be."

A constable is coming, dressed in his coxcomb helmet and long blue overcoat with a neat vertical line of shining buttons. He carries a hard wooden truncheon in his hand. He is watching the carriages rolling past, looking for his opportunity to approach.

"Irregulars!" hisses Malefactor. And in an instant they are gone.

When five o'clock comes, Sherlock wants to stay in the square; never go home. Why should he go home to sadness, to hopelessness, to Rose and Wilber Holmes?

Better to be here on the streets near the thrills and the successes, where he's seen so many fascinating and frightening things. He saw Lewis Carroll, one day, carrying his *Alice's Adventures in Wonderland* in his very hand; another time, Disraeli, the greatest politician in the land, strolling quietly through the Square; Anna Swan the Giantess with her head high above the crowd, the amazing high-rope star, Blondin, and the one and only Mr. Dickens, his black goatee streaked with gray, his eyes on fire. He's seen the Square packed with protestors shouting at the government to change its ways, and filled with citizens roaring for the feats of the Empire. He's seen the black-faced chimney sweeps, the deformed beggars, and the pickpockets of the streets. Why should he go home?

But he always goes. When Big Ben, the clock tower at the Parliament Buildings, strikes 5:00, he flies, intent on getting back before his parents, so they will think he's been to school. For many months now, he's been truant. In his heart, he knows they more than suspect him: they see right through him. It can't continue. If he doesn't go to school, he will have to work. The family needs his contribution. He will have to accept his lot among the poor working classes of London.

Dark clouds are gathering.

Sherlock realizes that his heart is racing, that it's been pumping faster since the moment he opened *The Illustrated Police News*. Something is burning inside him.

He looks down at the newspaper: he crushes it tightly, strangling the word *murder* in a fist.

A DARK PAST

Big Ben strikes 5:00. Sherlock starts to run, following the familiar route over the wide stone bridge, *The Police News* still in his hand.

He has it timed. Two hundred sprinting strides across the bridge through the crowds take less than two minutes. East along the brown Thames, past ominous old Clink Prison to Borough High Street, is a thousand fast footfalls: eight minutes. Borough is a wide thoroughfare and as respectable as Southwark gets, but his home is off it, seven narrow streets farther south, near a terrible neighborhood known as The Mint.

Dark, stone railway bridges loom here and there over the streets. The piercing screams of steam locomotives often cut through the air, making pedestrians jump out of their skins.

Sherlock sticks to the warren of alleys and lanes along Borough's west side, keeping up his speed so the urchins, the beggars, the thieves of the slums can't knock him down and rob him.

It starts to drizzle. A London day isn't complete without a little rain.

He always smells his neighborhood before he sees it: fish and vegetables being sold at the intersection near his street, sour odors wafting from the tanneries nearby, hanging rabbit meat, pigs' heads, or cold mutton at the local butcher shops. He hears familiar curses in the air.

As he nears home, his fear of being recognized grows. If anyone sees him, slows him down, he won't make it on time. He took too long reading about the murder, but he couldn't stop himself.

Folks around here know he should be in school and will tell his parents if they spot him. He drops his chin down to his chest as he rushes on, wishing he could withdraw his head into his neck-tied collar like a turtle.

"Sherlock!" a voice shouts.

It sounds like someone his age: maybe a schoolmate. He keeps running. But a little farther on, he slows when he sees a group of boys he knows, playing skittles in a lot where a building was recently knocked down, in preparation for another new rail line. The boys are using an old human skull for a ball, bowling it into bones they have set up as pins, all unearthed from a pauper's gravesite, and . . .

Suddenly Sherlock crashes headlong into something and goes sprawling off the foot pavement onto the street. He glances up.

It's Ratfinch.

He's the neighborhood fishmonger, and today he's carrying two barrels full of eels on his cart. They are tasty when fried over the fire with drippings, but they're slimy now, wriggling around on the boy as he lies on his back, stunned. His coat is drenched.

"Master 'olmes? . . . What in the . . . ? Ain't you supposed to be . . . ?" Ratfinch has a huge scar on his left cheek, made by a fishing hook. The wound cuts all the way across his face in a deep groove.

Sherlock springs to his feet, grasping at the eels, trying to grip the big slippery worms and drop them back into the monger's barrels – a passerby rights the containers on the street. The boy is growing frantic. Now he's *very late*. He mumbles an apology and escapes, wiping his coat with his hands as he scrambles away, praying the old material will dry quickly.

"Holmes!" yells one of the boys from the skittles game, rushing toward him. Sherlock lowers his head and runs.

Their home is just off the main thoroughfare, in a row of shops that line the road leading to the frightening lanes of The Mint. Almost everything is made of brick or stone here, but these buildings, built in the late 1600s, are all made of wood: the ground floor shops with bulging, latticed windows, the first floor flats above, with small, decaying insides.

He approaches their lodgings at a desperate sprint and slips down the little alley that turns off their street and goes along the back of the shops. It is barely wider than his scrawny shoulders. He whips past the back of the butcher's, the baker's, and then his own building, the old hatter's smells drifting out. He climbs over the crumbling brick wall at the rear. There is a rickety staircase a few steps away that rises to the only entrance to their flat. He ascends on the fly. At the top, on a sort of tiny landing, barely wide enough for a man to stand on, Sherlock can see back down the alley in the direction he has come. What he glimpses when he looks turns his face whiter than its usual hue: his parents, hand in hand, entering the passageway. They often meet on Borough and come home together. He is just seconds ahead!

The family door is never locked. No one would steal anything they have. His long white fingers fumble at the latch as his parents come closer. He presses his thumb down on the metal, lifting the little bar inside to release the catch. But he is too anxious, lets go too soon, and it catches again. He leans on the wooden door, but it won't open. He hears them talking, getting closer. He struggles with the latch once more. His hands are shaking. He calms himself, presses the latch down slowly, gently pushes the door open, and slips inside. The flat is a small room with a smaller one leading off to his right. The boards squeak as he rushes across the main room, throws himself on his little frame straw bed against the wall, and seizes one of his father's books from the shelf above him. He is still breathing hard.

The latch gently lifts. The door creaks open and closes.

"Sherlock? Are you home?"

"Yes, Mother."

"Hello, son."

"Father."

Wilberforce Holmes – tall, lean and dark – examines him closely. His powers of observation are at least as acute as his son's: his gift to him. But he doesn't need to be a detective to sense what is amiss about the boy today.

"What do I smell?" he asks suspiciously. "Fish?"

"Ratfinch is nearby," says Sherlock nonchalantly, getting up so he can put his back to his father. "I just passed him." The boy grimaces to himself, realizing that this doesn't make much sense. The fishmonger's smells, mixed with all the other odors outside, wouldn't penetrate these walls.

His father observes him. "Are you out of breath?"

"No."

How long can he keep his back turned? His coat is still wet in front from the eels, but only in front. Will they believe it's the rain? How often does it rain on just one side of your clothes?

"How was school?" continues his father.

"Instructive."

His parents don't smile. There is silence as they look at each other, still holding hands.

"So . . . what did you study today?" asks his mother, forcing a happier tone.

"Same old things."

Mr. Holmes has had enough. "Should I ask your headmaster?"

"No . . . don't . . . I . . . I was rushing home from over the river to get here first." He confesses. "I collided with Mr. Ratfinch."

The disappointment is written on their faces.

"At least try," pleads his mother as she sighs and undoes her purple bonnet, a fancy hat for a woman of her station, a relic now becoming worn, from her earlier life. Her face is still attractive, though the lines are deepening, and her hands are growing rougher.

An image of the murdered woman, as pretty as his mother once was, appears in his mind. Sherlock pushes it aside and tries to think only of Rose, long ago. He glances at the fading little painting they keep on their rough sideboard . . . his beautiful young mother, the nightingale.

He often imagines her in those golden days.

Her name was once Rose Sherrinford and she had been the jewel in her parents' life, their only daughter, destined for heaven on earth. The Sherrinfords were country squires with a mixture of French in their blood. Along with her refined education and beauty, Rose carried with her a dowry of many thousands of pounds, a prize for any properly placed young English gentleman. But she was a restless spirit who dreaded living an arranged life. She loved to sing and dreamt of joining The Royal Opera Company at Covent Garden, though she knew it was an "improper" role for a high-born young lady. All her parents would allow her was training. The best voice coaches in England molded her and soon she sang like an angel, but only at social gatherings at home. She memorized all the great roles, idolized the famous mezzo-sopranos, and never missed a production at the Opera House. She bristled at the way her parents caged her. But they were sure these feelings would pass – a man of position would sweep her away from all her unnatural inclinations.

Then the Jew arrived.

Wilber Holmes was a genius. Chemistry was his forte, but the mysteries of all the sciences were unlocked with mere flicks of his mind. Ornithology intrigued him the most. He loved the power of flight. But as the son of a poor immigrant Jew, an Ashkenazi from Eastern Europe at that, there was little opportunity to fly. Wilber's father had changed the family's very name to make them feel at home and proclaim their loyalty to England: *Holmes*. And he called his son Wilberforce ("It's unusual – be proud of the way it marks you.") after the great English believer in racial equality, and walked the boy to the Jews' Free School each day, prodding him to win top honors. But it wasn't enough. Despite Wilber's skill, the road to higher education – the chance to really get somewhere – looked blocked. In his youth during the 1840s, people of his race and social class were not allowed into the great schools of Oxford and Cambridge.

Still, the young man searched for a chance. He found one at The University College of London, a younger city school, and as he neared the end of a stellar student career, he became a teacher in training. *Professor Holmes*, he often wrote on scraps of paper, and smiled.

Then everything changed.

An admirer of his abilities took him to the opera. There he looked up from his seat to the nearest balcony and saw her, in a gleaming white box above him, her blonde hair shining and blue eyes glistening, the soaring violins of Rossini's *The Thieving Magpie* a perfect background for her beauty. She was mouthing every word, dreaming she was on that stage.

He couldn't help staring. Somehow, she felt his gaze. Soon she was looking back at a dark man with dark hair and eyes, the intelligence, the gentleness and kindness just glowing there. Her free spirit flew to him.

\

"You were at the front of your form when you tried. The headmaster wanted you for pupil teacher."

The boy shakes himself out of his daydream. His mother is still talking.

"You shall go out to work with your hands if you don't attend," adds his father sadly. "We pay much more than we can afford to keep you there, you know that. Most boys are gone well before your age."

"I'll . . . " he stammers, "I'll attend. Tomorrow."

Rose rests her bonnet on one of the hooks under the soot-smeared little window that faces out into the alley. She turns and puts her hands on her hips, fists balled on the frayed folds of her long cotton dress. It droops and hangs on her frame, bereft of any fashionable crinoline underneath to make it bloom. Her blonde hair is threaded with gray. She reaches out and cups Sherlock's face in her hands, searching his eyes, then kisses him.

"I'll find us something to eat."

She visits the markets at the end of the day, when you can get the pickings for pennies. She pulls a few carrots and an onion out of her basket, another half doorstep of bread, and two black-spotted potatoes. She sets them on the little wooden table in the center of the room where she prepares their meals. She will mix them for stew over the fire.

Wilber Holmes puts his coat on another hook, and loosens his necktie. He looks tired. He always tries to see the bright side of things, but his dark eyes often betray him when he tries to smile. He pulls his spectacles from a pocket, sits beside his son, and reaches for a book. There are a few dozen in a row. *British Birds* and *The Flight of Birds* are always nearest at hand. He must have read them a hundred times, but he can't stop. Most men spend their nights drinking in public houses on the nearby streets. Wilber Holmes has no use for such gin palaces. He flies into the skies with his birds.

Sherlock sits beside him without saying a word, racked with guilt about not attending school, but ambivalent about ever going back. His thoughts are still far away anyway, remembering the story of his parents' fateful meeting at the opera, the meeting that both made and destroyed his life.

After the last strains had played that night, the young Jew left slowly, while the privileged young woman rushed from her seat, anxious to tell her family about this latest Rossini spectacle. One sauntered one way outside the front doors, turning back to remember the opulence of where he'd been. The other burst out, searching for her carriage. The collision was a gentle one. He caught her in his arms.

It frightened his parents and infuriated hers. It was impossible, they told her. She didn't understand who she was. No Sherrinford could marry this Jew.

The young couple was amply warned.

After they eloped to Scotland, they came home to nothing. Her parents disowned her. His teaching opportunities at the university disappeared as mysteriously as he had once solved scientific problems.

And so they moved to Southwark, south of the Thames to the flat over the hatter's shop. She became the wife of an unemployed Jew of foreign origins and took jobs teaching children to sing in upper class houses, and when money became even shorter, taking in sewing at home. Wilber might have taught rudimentary science in an elementary school in the city, but the University College of London would never vouch for him, provide the "character" he needed. His father-in-law had seen to that. So, for a few years he tutored the sons of working men in his flat, then went farther south to work at a job that paid less than any school, but one he enjoyed, at The Crystal Palace, where he'd seen trained birds performing in great flocks for massive crowds. They needed a knowledgeable man to tend to their thousands of white doves: the Doves of Peace.

The couple stood by each other with little except their love. They had three children: Mycroft, born eight months after their marriage, Sherlock some seven years later, and then Violet – little Violet, who died before she reached the age of four.

Now the older boy was gone, employed in a lowly government job, reluctant to ever come home.

The middle child, the eccentric one, was left alone. He went to a Ragged School for destitute children when Rose and Wilber couldn't afford anything better, and to a National School when they almost could.

Sherlock loves his mother and father, and despises the life they have given him. He could have been *someone else*.

He hates what people do to each other. Why are prejudice and crime as constant as the yellow fog in this horrible and magnificent city?

Why would someone murder a beautiful lady in an alleyway in the dead of night?

OMENS FROM THE SKY

Wilber Holmes closes *The Flight of Birds* with a snap and tries to set the book back on the shelf. He settles for holding it on his lap. Then he tries to brighten things.

"Tell me about your day, son. What did you really do? I won't criticize."

"I went to Trafalgar Square."

"Again."

"Yes, sir."

"Anything of note?" Wilber sees the sensational publication clutched in his son's hands. It isn't the sort of newspaper that interests him.

"There was a terrible murder last night."

Wilber yawns and covers his mouth. "Again."

"This one was different."

"Anything else?"

"There were crows at the Square."

"Really?" Wilber's eyes light up and lock on Sherlock's. He twists around on the narrow bed. "You know, they're probably the smartest of all the birds, with the possible exception of their cousin, the raven. They have the largest brain-to-body ratio of the species."

Mrs. Holmes turns to them from the table where she is slicing the vegetables with an oversized butcher knife. "Crows always give me the shivers. They eat dead things; they make horrid sounds; they swoop around the heads of the witches in *Macbeth*."

"The burden of the carrion breed, dear, the black carrion breed, slyer than a fox. Some of my colleagues used to say that crows were able to pick out individual human beings and tell one of us from another. Now that's pretty clever."

Sherlock gets up and walks past the table. A big tin tub sits on it, half-filled with water, next to where his mother is working. He takes it down and sets it near the fire where she will need it. When she looks away for an instant, he snatches a thin shard of carrot, then opens the door and steps out onto the creaky little landing. The rain has stopped and darkness is falling. The gaslights from Borough High slightly light the thin fog. All of the buildings on their street are jammed together and each has a tiny, walled backyard. A dying tree, the only one on the block, almost fills the hatter's. In it sit two black birds.

The crows. They've followed him.

Their dark feathers look oily and tattered.

"*Corvus corone*," says his father, standing behind him in the doorway. "Fine birds, really. Fine little rascals. They mate for life."

A rock whizzes through the yard toward the crows. They lift off at once and are gone. Another rock arches into the air after them.

"You lot!" shouts Sherlock, leaning dangerously far over the frail railing to find the culprits. Down the alley, he sees two little boys glaring back at him. "Leave off!"

"Black devils and Jews is the curse of our land!" shrieks one as they scurry away.

"Come in," says Rose softly, who had stepped out to see the birds. "Your meal will be ready soon."

Sherlock spots the crows in the distance. The London sky is growing darker. The black birds vanish into it.

Something occurs to him.

Inside, he finds *The Illustrated Police News*, opens it, and looks at the drawing. There is the poor woman lying on the cobblestones. But what is that? At the top of the picture, not far from the corpse, the artist has drawn something dark with several strokes of the pen.

Sherlock bends his head down and examines the little figure in the shadows.

It is a crow.

THE MURDERER

Sherlock starts out with every intention of going to school the next morning, but the noisy crowds seem to impel him toward the city like a strong wind. Just one more day, maybe two, then he'll go back for good. He follows his route toward Trafalgar Square, glancing back from time to time, afraid he's being trailed. There are many would turn him in: a teacher, a local hawker, even the old hatter with his cloudy red eyes and scowling face.

But over the river a treasure awaits him. Eyes alert as always, he spies a copy of the morning's *Police News*, jammed under one of the outside seats on the top of an omnibus, clattering through the traffic toward him. The paper has been left up there and no one on the bus is paying the slightest attention to it. The driver is clutching the reins and the ladies inside are looking straight ahead into the noisy intersection. How can anyone abandon such spectacular information? He slips off the foot pavement right into the flow of horses and vehicles, puts a foot on the conductor's platform at the rear, and executes a little jump to nab the paper. Not one of the whiskered faces under the tall black hats turns. Tucking it into his coat, he vanishes back into the traffic and crosses to the north side before looking at his prize.

He loves this stretch of Fleet Street where the big newspapers have their offices. He's seen grim Mr. Gladstone twice, enemy of Disraeli and once a Chancellor of the Exchequer, his big sideburns puffed out, his walking stick in hand, a perfect top hat on his well-developed head. And last week he spotted The Great Farini, the man who walked over Niagara Falls on a high wire. His flying-trapeze protégé, the bullet-boy El Niño, was by his side.

But today he doesn't see anyone who matters, because the front page of the paper stops him in his tracks. "MURDERER FOUND!" it proclaims. There under the headline is a crude drawing of a young man named Mohammad Adalji, depicted with a big, hooked nose and nearly black skin. "It seems an Arab did the dirty deed," reads the first line. Sherlock scans the story, " . . . lives not five blocks from the scene . . . found with a butcher knife . . . blood . . . to be bound over today at approximately 9:00 a.m. . . . the Old Bailey Courthouse."

Sherlock had heard the faint bong of Big Ben just as he snatched the paper. Nine o'clock. The Old Bailey: it's only minutes away.

He turns and runs.

The crowd is still gathering when he arrives, spilling out into the road waiting for the murderer. Sherlock jostles his way up to the front, hearing men and women cursing the Arab and his horrible crime. Some clutch rotting vegetables and even broken bricks in their hands. Nearly a dozen Bobbies, London's respected policemen, stand nervously nearby, gripping their rock-hard, black truncheons in their hands.

On the north side of the Old Bailey looms infamous Newgate Prison, where "the Jew," Fagin, was held in one of Sherlock's favorite novels, Mr. Dickens' *Oliver Twist*. The scaffold is always placed directly in front of the main doors of its dreary, windowless exterior. These streets are packed on hanging days – enormous audiences stretch as far as one can see, the best spots reserved at top price, Mr. Dickens often somewhere in the crowd.

Soon, two thick dray horses pull a big coach up the street: the frightening *Black Maria* used to transport the worst villains. Its ominous appearance has the effect of throwing coal on fire and the mob's mood instantly grows angrier.

"That's 'im!"

"Get 'im!"

"MURDERER!"

As Adalji descends the dark wagon from the rear, manacled at his hands and feet, shoved roughly forward by the Old Bailey's jailers, an onslaught of filthy projectiles is launched at him. One strikes him in the face and he lowers his head, another hits him in the groin and he grimaces and bends over. The jailers drag him toward the gate, stretching out his arms almost as if to expose him to the crowd. Sherlock sees his face. It shocks him. He wonders if Mohammad Adalji has even reached eighteen. His skin is lighter than in the drawing, his nose smaller, and he looks terrified.

The Arab's eyes wildly survey the crowd, reflecting the hatred he sees. He notices Sherlock, and glimpses sympathy. Instinctively, he turns and attempts to take a step. A big man in the crowd reaches out and trips him. The Arab tries to keep his balance, but another knocks him down. He almost lands on Sherlock. His head is facedown on one of the boy's worn, heavily polished boots. As he rises to his feet, their eyes meet. There are tears streaked on the Arab's cheeks.

"*I didn't do it!*"

The police pull the Arab away. One of them notices the boy to whom the criminal has spoken and glares at Sherlock with suspicion. The constable says something to his partner. Then he glances into the sky.

Crows are circling.

The Arab sees them too. An expression of horror comes over his face.

"Sod off, crow devils!" shouts the big man, as he fires a rotten apple at the biggest black bird.

On his way to Trafalgar Square, Sherlock can't get the Arab's words out of his mind. He'd known the scene would be sensational, but it had sickened him. He can't tell a single soul, of course. If anyone asks, he'll say that it served the murderer right. But he keeps wondering. Did that frightened boy *really* do it?

Lost in thought, he walks on to the Strand through the ancient Temple Bar Gate, where long ago, traitors' severed heads were once displayed.

"Don't I know you?"

A wind-worn face is suddenly inches in front of his, sending a cloud of fish-breath up his nostrils.

"Don't I *know* you?!" it shouts.

Sherlock's heart nearly stops.

Then he realizes who it is: a one-legged lunatic he's often seen here near Charing Cross, his filthy clothes held together with strings and pins he's scavenged on the river-banks, begging from pedestrians by exaggerating his lunacy. Word is he's a Crimean War veteran and the Bobbies seldom have the heart to take him away. Drool drips from his toothless gums as his vacant eyes stare into Sherlock's. The boy steps adroitly past him.

At Morley's Hotel, he looks both ways into the mass of traffic that claps along the stones, then darts across Trafalgar, artfully dodging the wagons and hansom cabs, horses with riders, and vendors with their carts. He looks back. The crows have returned. Three are perched on the hotel to resume their watch, two others atop the glorious golden lion above the gates of Northumberland House.

The boy leans against the carved stone wall that runs around the exterior of the main part of the square, turning his back on the crows, thinking about the Arab. Every now and then he pulls a rusty brush from a coat pocket and makes sure his straight black hair is perfectly in place.

He loves to watch birds almost as much as people: cardinals, finches, robin redbreasts, magpies, anything. Most of all, he likes to watch them fly. "That's the one thing they do that human beings wish we could do," his father often tells him. "We'd all love to fly. It would free us from the bonds of Earth."

Sometimes, he's spotted hot air balloons drifting over the tall buildings and church spires of the city like they've floated away from some strange dream of the future. It isn't truly flying, but it is close. Oh, to be up there!

Feeling restless, he gets to his feet and makes his way across the square toward the Art Gallery. He walks up the big steps. He feels compelled to come here where he can see so many rich folks. Rich is something he will never be. All he can do is watch and dream.

He knows that nearly a third of the children in London don't attend school, and very few go after the age of twelve. Most are put to work or worse. Yet he is still in the cramped National and Foreign Society School on Snowfields Road near the London Bridge Railway Station. Three damp rooms on three floors: one for the little children, one for upper form girls, and a big one for boys. The last is at the top of the stairs with a high ceiling (beckoning you to stare up and drift into a better world), where the masters, monitors, and all the students also gather for assemblies. He has been in school for seven years, his parents insisting that he read better than the others, cipher better . . . think better. But there is a ceiling on his future lower than the one in his classroom.

He thinks of his earlier days, in the dirty Ragged School in Lambeth, sitting in one of the many rows at his narrow wooden desk, beside other miserable pupils. He is fortunate to be gone from there. Unlike those destitute children, he at least has some sort of future, some expectations. In the summers he's helped the old hatter in the shop under their flat, adding what he can to the family income; it was said he did well. He may become a full-time shop assistant some day, a clerk, or a teacher; nothing better.

"But look at Disraeli," his father often tells him. "He will be prime minister one day, mark my words. Other Jews are getting places too. They let us sit in Parliament now. It's 1867! When I was a boy things were much worse."

But Benjamin Disraeli isn't the sort of Jew that Sherlock is, or like any he knows. Those who succeed, like the Rothschilds and a recent Lord Mayor of London, have never lived in the slums of Southwark or Whitechapel; their blood isn't mixed; their parents haven't suffered a great fall. In fact, Disraeli comes from a middle-class family and was baptized in the Church of England: his life has been filled with opportunities. And yet the boy recently saw the great man drawn with a grotesquely long nose and caricatured as Fagin in a copy of *Punch* magazine he found in the streets.

The boys at school call Sherlock "Judas," or "Old Clothes," the name for conniving Jewish street vendors. He is a loner to begin with, doesn't like to talk: it seems he just reads and thinks. He wears preposterous suits with waistcoats (bought "passed on" at a market), threadbare but as clean as he can make them, his only way to be somebody, though it separates him even more. He's had a few fights at Snowfields. He won't give in or let other boys go unpunished for mean things they say. But some still taunt him. They resent his many first-place finishes, his razor-sharp mind.

One fight still bothers him more than any other. It happened nearly a year ago. The school bully had teased him so mercilessly that he'd challenged the boy on the street. A big crowd gathered. His opponent was a hulking, eleven-stone pure-English lad. Sherlock went down with the first blow, was pounced upon, his thin arms pinned until they nearly snapped on the pavement. The boy spit on him and slapped his face as the others looked on and cheered.

"'elpless, ain't you, Judas? Absolutely 'elpless!" cried the boy. "You can rub your grades in our gobs and wear those clothes and take those snooty ways, but you still ain't goin' anywhere remarkable. You're pinned down, you are, like you should be!"

When the large boy finally relented and climbed off, Sherlock wouldn't get up. The crowd stood and looked down at him. He lay there, flat on his back on the street, until everyone was gone.

He'd been absent from school maybe once a week before that fight, but since then his record had drastically declined. He tries to attend: knows he owes it to his parents. But he can't. Education *can* get you somewhere, but where has it gotten his father?

A goldfinch is flying by against the gray clouds. The air has cooled and it looks like rain again. Sherlock is thinking about the murder.

The new *Illustrated Police News* is still in his pocket. He hasn't read much of it yet, just the headline and a few words about Mohammad Adalji. He pulls it out and turns to the second page. There the lurid drawing has been reproduced from the day before.

The blood. The woman. That crow.

The story flows onto the next page where another picture of the victim is drawn for the reader. Her pretty eyes look just like his mother's in the little painting back in their flat.

The woman's identity has still not been revealed. He reads on.

It is an open-and-shut case. There is no doubt that the Arab did it. The police are certain. An old detective named Lestrade is in charge.

> We found him not far from the scene, blood on his hands, a butcher's knife concealed under his coat. She wasn't a wealthy woman, but well turned out. This villain must have thought she had money. There are signs that he took her coin purse, though we haven't recovered it. He must have ditched it somewhere. Remnants were found at the scene. We will talk to him, talk to him smartly. The purse shall be found. And he will swing for this.

Further down the page Sherlock reads that the Arab's trial will take place in about three weeks. Punishment will swiftly follow. The clock has begun ticking on Mohammad Adalji's life.

When Big Ben strikes 5:00, it sounds like a distant gong in another county to Sherlock. He gets up and walks mechanically toward the river. Before he's gone far he notices that the crows are nearby again. Two of them are flying above him. But then they veer away. He decides to follow. He should go straight home, but something inside urges him to go with them.

They are flying toward the oldest part of London, the city proper, the area inside the ancient London Wall, where spooky little streets wind around like snakes slithering into stone burrows. It is filled with banks these days, but it's where the Romans once lived, where the Vikings and Saxon lords ruled, where witches told gruesome tales, and wretched medieval men and women were whipped and tortured in public.

The crows fly, then roost, and then move on. Following them gives him an uneasy feeling . . . like he's with the devil's birds.

Where are they going? Where do they stay at night? Usually they find tall trees.

Before long the Tower of London with its famous prison is to his right down by the Thames. Soon after it slips from sight, the crows start flying lower.

He is a long way east now, in a working-class area. There are rag-and-bone shops, candle makers, costermongers and their carts everywhere: an immigrant neighborhood even poorer than his own. This wide road isn't so bad, but down the smaller streets he sees desperate people walking about, many in bare feet, others lying against soot-stained buildings. He sees Jews too, crowds of them, some selling clothes, yes, with long beards and piles of hats on their heads. Languages he can't understand fill the air.

There are no gas lamps down these back-ways. Soon the sunlight will grow dimmer; the famous London fog, beginning to settle in, will get thicker. People are rushing home, leaving the main road. He goes by a street named Goulston.

He shouldn't be here. Sinister-looking men pass, eyeing him.

"Easy mark," he thinks he hears a dusky one in a sailor's cap murmur to another.

He keeps his eye on the crows. But suddenly they vanish. They drop somewhere to his left, just a short distance ahead. He is beginning to feel lost. The side streets here seem darker, like wolf dens.

He stops at a narrow one . . . Old Yard . . . his best guess as to where the birds have gone. There are two shops on either side of the entrance and their upper stories, grim-looking lodgings, are built right across and over the little street.

He takes a deep breath and ventures down it, his heart pounding.

It is like being in a tunnel. The sides of the two-storey buildings lean out over the road, cutting off the setting sun. Filthy children dressed in rags crawl out from nowhere, begging with pleading eyes and outstretched hands.

Others have lined up their pathetic shoes on the grim, dirty footpaths, hoping for a sale. They smell as if they've bathed in cesspools. Many cough horribly, and their skin looks green. These are the sorts of areas where four or five families live in single rooms.

It is time to leave. Past time.

But then he spots the crows down an empty alley.

What are they doing?

He can barely see them. They've landed right on the ground. They are bobbing about on the cobblestones deep in the alley, hardly visible in the dimming light. He looks at the street name on the brick building at the corner. It seems familiar. He isn't sure why.

Sherlock hesitates. He is in an area his parents don't allow him to even go near, let alone enter. He is beyond late. They'll kill him when he gets home.

He hears the crows muttering.

He turns down the alley.

The wooden doors on either side are boarded up. They look like entrances to stables that haven't been used for a long time. There is an eerie silence. He takes each step with great care, as if someone might leap out from behind those doors and pounce.

He hears the sound of caws through the yellow fog.

Why are the crows on the ground?

He advances. They don't move. Now he can almost step on them. They are pecking at something on the cobblestones. He crouches down. The ground is gray, but it looks different where the crows are, as if it is stained . . . red.

Then he remembers why he recognized this little lane's name. He has read it many times in the newspapers over the last few days.

That red stain is human blood.

He is standing on the *very* spot where the woman was murdered!

VIOLIN LAND

He runs from the East End with all his might, runs as if he were trying to get away from all the hatred in the world, the brutal ways people treat each other, from whomever it is who murdered that woman.

In bed that night he can't sleep. He keeps thinking about the scene in the alley: the black lane, crows pecking at the cobblestones, the blood. He had felt watched, as if someone were standing somewhere in that mist, following his every move.

Now he feels ashamed. Why had he been *so* afraid? Would he stand up against evil if he could help? Would he do something? He's just a boy – a mixed-up mixture of a boy. But what if that Arab didn't do it? What if an innocent man is going to hang? What if someone is going to get away with something much worse than taunts in a schoolyard . . . with murder?

No one is going to do anything about it.

He rises in the morning with dark circles under his eyes. His mother would have noticed. But she has gone to teach three singing lessons: one in Belgravia, two in Mayfair.

His father will leave soon too. He walks five miles to The Crystal Palace every morning, and back again in the evening. He is sitting at their little table, staring blankly while he takes his breakfast, a bowl of porridge and a warm cup of tea in front of him. He wears his spectacles; his old black frock coat is as clean as Rose can make it, his black beard neatly trimmed.

When Sherlock arrived late last night, he had admitted to his parents that he'd been in central London again (though he didn't say where he'd gone later). He asked for one more day of freedom and then he'd go to school every day. He promised.

"Good morning, Father," says the boy. He looks in their little mirror to make sure his hair is in place.

Wilber responds without lifting his head.

"Sherlock. Sleep well?"

"I did, thank you." He sits down.

"I feel that you have a question."

His father is like that. He has a sixth sense about everything.

"Remember we talked about crows yesterday?"

"Yes," Wilber's eyes focus and he looks at his son. "Yes, I do."

"You said they were smart," says the boy, leaning forward.

"Undoubtedly."

"That they were carrion eaters."

"Unfortunately. Tends to make folks a little prejudiced about them."

"That they can recognize people. What else?"

Wilber takes his bowl to the shelf. His mind is beginning to shift to his day's work. "What exactly do you mean?"

"Can they do anything else that's unusual?"

Wilber had turned toward the door, but he stops and smiles as he looks back at his son. Lately, he and Sherlock haven't had long conversations like they used to, when he would impart all the knowledge he could to his son, training him to use his brain as his weapon in life. It is wonderful to hear the boy asking questions again.

"Well, some of my colleagues believe that crows can talk, or shall we say . . . communicate well."

"What else?" Sherlock stands up, and approaches his father. He doesn't want to eat anything this morning, and intends to go as soon he can.

"Let me see . . . they come from a whole family of birds who like shiny things."

"Shiny things?"

"They seem to have fairly well ordered brains and if anything is out of place they are drawn to it. Shiny things stand out. They go to them like magnets." A slight frown creases his brow. "That doesn't help their reputation either. They are considered thieves. A little advice to you when in the company of crows, my boy: don't leave anything of value lying about, or they might just relieve you of it." He laughs.

They are silent for a moment. Wilber turns to go again.

"I've read that they're omens of evil," says Sherlock.

His father stops in his tracks.

"People do evil," he replies decisively, "not birds."

Once Sherlock gets over the river that morning, he keeps north through the narrow streets. As he rounds a corner he notices something moving in the shadows up ahead where a lane leads off a roadway, and then a little army files out, like rats coming up from the sewers.

His pulse quickens.

Usually, if he sees the Irregulars, he tries to steer clear of them. They seldom let him pass without some sort of violence, no matter what he does or says. If they catch him far off a main thoroughfare, his chances dim. They seem to hate him. But it isn't because of his Jewish blood. No, they have Jews in their fold. It is the blue in his veins. They sense that he isn't from the street, not truly. It is acceptable that Malefactor is so well spoken, after all he is the brains of their operation, has some mysterious past he won't speak of, and most importantly, delivers what they need in the underworld. But not the half-Jew. He is neither with them nor against them.

The gang leader, as bright as a new English guinea, knows all about Holmes just by looking at him. It is curious though, Sherlock also senses that somewhere deep in that twisted mind the other boy respects him. The feeling is mutual. The criminal thoughts in Malefactor's head are always magnificently conceived.

Sherlock nervously stands his ground. He wants to talk this time.

They are running right at him. Malefactor stops. He holds up his hand. The army grinds to a halt. There are thirteen of them altogether – their boss likes that number. They dress well, but are dirty and ragged, in a soiled display of soft felt hats, billycocks and caps, graying white linen shirts, and grimy silk neckties, having stolen everything they own – catching young Londoners alone and stripping them bare is a specialty of theirs – that and picking rich pockets. Hanging days are excellent for business. Sherlock has long since detected their backgrounds: seven of them Irish (including both bully lieutenants, Grimsby and Crew), two Welsh, a Scot, and two English Jews. Every one of them is an orphan or the child of workhouse parents, raised in rookeries or on the streets. All this is betrayed to Sherlock in the things they say and the way they say them. But their boss, the eldest by at least two years, is different. No child of a rookery speaks like him.

"Master Sherlock Holmes, I perceive."

"Malefactor," the boy says calmly.

"You want to talk?" The outlaw can read his mind.

"It's about the murder."

"That again?"

"Yes. Any word?"

"You'll warrant a major beating if you ask me that one more time."

"The Arab didn't do it," offers Sherlock bravely.

"A reasonable guess," replies Malefactor as he smoothes out his long black coat.

"Your world can't be any safer with a murderer on the loose."

"He isn't on the loose," says the thief without thinking.

"Oh?"

Malefactor looks like he's let the cat out of the bag.

"Move along, Sherlock Holmes." He glances over his shoulder toward his little thugs, nodding at Grimsby and Crew, who step forward. They love to beat on their victims, and both carry iron-hard hickory sticks for the purpose. Dark Grimsby likes to talk, blond Crew says little. They grin maliciously at the slender boy.

"If he turns and walks now, no hand shall strike him," says Malefactor. The lieutenants' shoulders sag.

Sherlock has noticed that the boss's slight Irish accent grows stronger when he is irritated. The two eye each other. They are both tall boys: skinny with large heads, though the leader has nearly an inch on the half-breed truant, his forehead bulges where Holmes' is flat, and his eyes are sunken while Sherlock's peer out. They both have a way of constantly looking about, suspiciously turning their heads – Malefactor the reptile, Sherlock the hawk. Their hair, an identical coal-black, is combed as perfectly as they can manage.

Malefactor first saw the boy on the streets many months ago and picked him out as different, drawn to him as if he were something shiny. The thug couldn't resist harassing him, but has yet to allow his followers to truly do him harm.

Sherlock turns and walks.

He is half a block away when a rotten tomato, fired like a bullet, catches him flush and splat on the back of his neck. His head turns like a falcon's. But they are gone.

He stands still for a few seconds. "Curse you!" he finally blurts, frantically wiping the red slime from his coat. "I'll never get this clean!"

"No *and* shall strike 'im!" echoes a voice from around a corner, trailing off, laughing maniacally as it fades into the London day.

He reads the papers again that morning. There is nothing new. The police have made up their minds. It strikes him that they think in straight lines and never have new ideas. He sits in the center of Trafalgar Square, among the tourists and the pigeons, stealing the odd chunk of bun from the fat gray birds. From time to time, he dips his necktie in one of the fountains and scours angrily at the red stain on his collar, until he nearly scrubs through the cloth.

The Irregulars don't know who murdered the woman. He can tell. But they know something. At least Malefactor does. There is no one on the streets of London more cunning than that constantly calculating boy. His minions not only fear him, but accept him as their better. Sherlock doesn't just imagine that Malefactor is of higher stock, he knows it. There's an indisputable clue: that long black coat with tails. Though it is tattered and frayed, the gang leader wears it every day, as if he prizes it deeply, not as if he's stolen it.

His chimneypot hat, his walking stick: those he sets down in alleys without thinking twice. But Sherlock has seen him cleaning his coat and tails in a rain barrel when he thinks others aren't looking, has watched him caress it and smooth it as he talks. Long ago, that coat belonged to someone of some social status. There are secrets within its folds.

Malefactor indeed has been blessed with more brain-power than the others. Nothing in London escapes his notice. He knows *something* about the Whitechapel murder.

But what? What else *is* there to know?

Sherlock casts his mind back to the scene from last night, his vivid imagination reproducing it almost perfectly. And as he does, he realizes something. The crows . . . they *weren't* staying on the blood stain! They were moving around, as if they were *looking* for something, as if . . .

"Sherlock."

Someone has spotted him, even though his head was down. It's a warm woman's voice, unrecognizable for an instant, as he suddenly awakes from his thoughts and leaps to his feet.

"Sherlock, it's just me," Rose laughs. "Don't be sur-prised. I knew I'd find you on this very spot. Remember, I was giving lessons in Mayfair today? It's not far from here." She motions to the west. She is wearing one of her best muslin dresses trimmed with lace, preserved as well as pos-sible from her other life. It had once been ivory white.

"Mother . . . I . . . "

"This is your last day away from school, correct?"

The boy nods.

"I want us to walk out together tonight," says Rose.

She sits down beside him and takes one of his long white hands in hers.

He knows what she means. She wants to go to the opera. They've gone many times before. She's been taking him for as long as he can remember. He is sure she brought him there in her arms, around to the back of the Royal Opera House in Covent Garden, just a short walk from Trafalgar. They slip into the shadows and go to her spot, a place where a coal grate opens on to the street and they can crouch and hear the music as if they are right in the seats. As he listens, she tells him the story of each opera, slowly and clearly, with tears in her eyes.

They sit in the Square that late afternoon, talking. He can smell the beer on her breath.

His mother's conversation is never about the past: always about what has happened that very day. Today, she begins with the big homes that she's just been in.

"The first was in Belgravia and it belongs to a duke."

She knows it will interest him and describes every inch of the ornate dwelling: its glittering front door, its glowing chandeliers, and the well-born lady who lives there . . . and never once deigned to say "Hello."

"The other house was in Mayfair," she continues.

The gentleman was home. He had a ruddy, red face, a long red goatee, and a rough way of talking. Everything he said was addressed to the servants. He never once spoke to his wife. He was so rude and ill-mannered, especially for a man whose spouse is related to the queen.

"He kept staring at me. Or at least I thought he did. He had the most peculiar eyes. One seemed so different from the other: some eyes are like that. Examine them, Sherlock, and you'll see. One eye was alive . . . and the other looked dead."

The sun is setting by the time they make their way up the Strand and then north toward Covent Garden. The market has closed for the day. Flower petals lie on the muddy ground, big torn baskets are scattered about, the shouts of costermongers and piemen have faded away. They cross the open area toward the back of the big opera house, a magnificent, white stone building.

Rose Holmes has a routine. She goes round to the front entrance, the part with the tall pillars that look out on Bow Street, then crosses the road and stands on the foot pavement, just south near the dim blue lights of the police station. She always takes Sherlock's hand, even now when he is thirteen, and squeezes it unconsciously while she watches.

The carriages pull up, one after the other. The famous people, the rich folk, step down, top hats shining, diamond stickpins glittering, silk dresses flowing. The boy performs his mental exercise as he watches; he observes and deciphers the life stories of each gentleman and lady.

Bobbies stand by, observing too, but they never watch the upper classes. It's the others who gain their attention. Sherlock catches their eyes several times and each time looks away.

Before the big doors are closed on the last grand couple, Rose yanks her son across the street. They steal down the north side of the Opera House and dart under a little wrought-iron staircase at the back of the massive building. It leads to a secret entrance, used by the singing stars. The little dark door is camouflaged with ivy, and the coal grate, hidden under the stairs, provides an opening into the building. They might as well be in the front row.

They huddle on the ground, Rose's dress in the mud, but she doesn't care. She puts an arm around Sherlock.

The music begins.

A cry escapes from her lips. It's *The Thieving Magpie*. Now he knows why she wanted to come tonight.

First the overture thunders, commencing with rolling drums, the sounds of an execution: the execution of a young girl. But his mother says nothing. She is waiting. Then she sighs.

Violins.

"They tell us," she often says, "of the tragedies of life."

She calls it violin land. It is the place she goes when she hears them. Her son knows what she means. He can feel it too. There are no instruments like them. Violins are sad; they are strong; they tell the truth. When they are slow, they make you cry. When they are fast, they press you forward, push you into the struggle of life.

"*Bah a bah, pa pa pa . . . Bah a bah, pa pa pa . . .*" She sings gently, to the sound of the swirling strings, the sound of the magpie darting through the air, heading toward its treasure.

Rose tells the story, her voice musical and gentle over the beautiful strains. In his mind, Sherlock can see the brilliant hall inside: the lit stage, the tiers of balconies, the rich red velvet seats, the magnificent silver chandeliers. And he can see the story.

"A magpie flies innocently through the air on its merry way at the opening of another day. It sees something shining through a window in an elegant home. It darts down. It's a spoon, a sparkling silver spoon worth more than its little brain can imagine. It lights on the sill. It looks around. It steals the spoon and flies away. The next day, the lady of the house is inconsolable. Someone has stolen one of her pure silver spoons. It must be one of the servants! A beautiful young girl, poor as a field mouse, happened to be working in the room when the spoon was taken. The lady accuses her. She is arrested. It is an open-and-shut case. She is sentenced to die. Her day of execution approaches . . . "

Rose Holmes never gives away the ending. Her son knows what will happen, but she never breathes a word of it, no matter how many times they listen. They huddle in the darkness until the last note is played. Then they leave like thieves, moving through the shadows back out to Bow Street, down to the river, and home.

Wilber is waiting. He knows where they've been. He takes his wife in his arms and holds her while she sobs. Then he puts her to bed.

The boy sits at the table. Sherlock Holmes doesn't cry, not about anything, ever.

"*The Thieving Magpie*," says his father, shaking his head, as he comes out and sits down. They are both quiet for a moment.

"What family do magpies belong to?" asks the boy suddenly.

Wilber smiles at him: "They're corvidae. The corvid family. There are jays, nutcrackers, ravens, and of course, your friends the crows."

The instant his father mentions the crows, an idea bursts into his head – Sherlock wonders why he hasn't thought of it before. He sits, dead silent, his mind far away.

His father is used to this sort of behavior. Sherlock is a strange lad. Most boys his age have herds of friends – he doesn't have one. Every now and then, right in the middle of a conversation, he'll slip into these silent stretches and float away. The boy will sit back, his lids nearly closed, and drift off. Wilber stands up, ruffles his son's hair, and slips off to bed in the side room.

Sherlock fixes his hair and rises to his feet. He moves to the back door, opens and closes it silently, and flies down the wooden stairs.

On the dark streets, he starts to run.

He is headed back over the bridge to the part of the city where the narrow streets wind through the fog like snakes . . . to that little lane with the bloodstain.

6

FIRST CLUE

The crows had been looking for something. He is sure of it.

Something shiny!

He is all the way to London Bridge before fear catches up with him. What in the world is he doing? It will soon be past midnight. He's never been out of doors in the city at this hour. The bridge is almost deserted. Nearly all the boats are docked: just an odd one floats on the black water. Above the endless crowds of shadowy buildings eerily lit by gas, he can see the dome of St. Paul's to the west, the evil Tower to the east. That poor woman was murdered at about this hour, down that narrow lane deep in the East End. He shudders to think of being there in the dead of night . . . *exactly* where he is going.

London is a dream past midnight: a nightmare. He leans against the bridge's stone balustrades, feeling terrified, and imagining the desperate people who must inhabit the night. Dim reflections of the bridge's lamps quiver on the water, and other than the distant blasts of a few steam whistles, it is frighteningly silent. He waits for something to come out of the fog.

Before long, it does. There are footsteps.

Someone is emerging in the darkness.

It is an old woman, dressed in shades of black, her clothes so worn that they seem to be patched together. Her hair hangs in strings, her face is like a mask. Beside her walks a child in a dirty sheet. No, not a child: it is a man, or an animal, dark-faced and about three feet tall, with crude juggling clubs in its hands. She has it by a chain. The hag looks at Sherlock and grins. Then the two figures disappear into the fog, floating, their near-silent steps moving slowly away. He hears the woman laugh. Or is it that thing by her side? It is an animal sound: a hyena's cry.

The little hairs stand up on Sherlock's arms; his flesh is tingling.

He has to make a choice: go forward or retreat home. He thinks of the school bully sitting on him, telling him he's helpless. He thinks of the young Arab's face, the fear in it, of him swinging from a rope on a scaffold in front of a huge crowd outside Newgate Prison. The people are cheering. They hate him. Three weeks and that will be the scene.

Sherlock steps away from the wall.

He is going to Whitechapel.

He walks with trepidation into the old part of the city: more people emerge out of the mists like cast members from dark operas. Their numbers grow as he moves east. Most are as strange as the old woman and her wretched companion: a ghostly parade of grotesque creatures, frail as skeletons, ragged as goats. A moaning, white-haired beggar clings to him for a while. He encounters gentlemen too, drunk as lords, staggering home in fine evening clothes, preyed upon by pickpockets who rob without breaking stride. Women circle on street corners under the hissing lamps, wearing dresses pulled down at the top and turned up at the bottom, red paint on their lips. Farther east they are poorer, older, and dirtier. Some look at the boy and laugh.

Malefactor is out there somewhere hard at work, stealing his way through life: surviving, providing for his nasty followers.

It seems to take Sherlock forever to get where he is going. There aren't as many lights in the East End. He meets fewer people, sees some lying on the footpaths or sitting against black buildings, unable to get lodgings for the night. There are sounds in the mist. Under each dim glow of light, he stops and looks back: just shadows, it seems, and voices like echoes.

Finally, he finds Old Yard Street, and realizes it has no gas lamps.

He walks into the darkness; soon the alley appears dimly to his left. He stands still for a moment. Then he turns down it.

Footsteps behind!

He swings around. No one. Silence.

He moves again, his boots sounding like cannons on the cobblestones. The bloodstain is somewhere near. The fog seems very heavy. He drops down on his hands and knees and edges forward, his eyes inches from the ground.

There it is.

His fingers are right on the stain. He casts his mind back again. He sees the crows once more at the scene. The picture appears in his mind in two dimensions, as clear as a stereographic view. There they are! One is on the stain, yes, but the other is a carriage length away, near a damp wall. It isn't pecking like the one on the blood. Its dark head moves with a different motion. It is doing something with its beak . . . *digging!*

Sherlock crawls forward. His eyes are becoming more accustomed to the darkness. He can see the spot where the bird was digging just ahead. He reaches it . . . a rubble of bricks, probably dumped here by a tradesman.

Something moves, right near his head. He sucks in his breath. It makes a scratching sound.

A black bird is an arm's length from his face. It spreads out its torn, evil-looking feathers for an instant, as if to fly. Then it stops and stares at him. He can see the intelligence in its dark eyes. It tips its head, regards him once more, and lifts off.

It vanishes.

Sherlock turns back to the rubble and at that instant the fog lifts slightly in the alleyway, the moon shines through, and he sees something. It glitters in the stones.

Something shiny. It is nearly buried. He moves a crumbling brick.

Then he shudders and almost falls face-first into the rubble.

It's a body! And it's buried under the bricks!

An eye is staring up at him . . . a human eye.

Steeling himself for the sight of a corpse, he takes a deep breath and works as fast as he can, moving more pieces. But the body's head must be tilted sideways, because no matter how hard he digs, only one eye is evident.

Then he realizes *exactly* what he has found. It isn't a corpse. It is *just* an eye. A single human eye is buried in the rubble a half dozen steps from the spot where the woman was murdered.

Then he realizes something else. It isn't real. It is a glittering, glass eyeball. Sherlock stares at it. It stares back. Flecks of blood are splattered on the iris. He picks it up.

Footsteps again!

He is sure this time. Absolutely sure! And they are coming toward him. He closes his fingers over the eyeball, rises to his feet, and starts to run.

"Boy!" he hears a gruff voice shout.

Perched up above in the night, the crow lets out a scream.

Sherlock runs in the darkness. He hears violins . . . from another Rossini opera he and his mother have heard many times. They are the galloping, charging, fleeing, escaping violins of *The William Tell Overture*. Sherlock puts his head back, pumps his fists and lets his long legs take him. The music powers him: out the alleyway, past a dark, ghostly man with a gas lamp reaching out to grab him. But Sherlock eludes him and is gone in an instant, around the corner, past a parked black coach on Whitechapel, then down the street and on the double toward the ancient stone arches of London Bridge.

"Boy!"

The cry fades as he flees. He barely notices the night people this time. His mind is fixed on home. He holds the eye tightly in his hand as he sprints off the bridge, through Southwark, away from the street, and onto the lane that leads to the back stairs of the family flat. When he gets there, he goes up three steps at a time.

Who was that? Who was standing in that alley where the woman was murdered?

His shaking hands open the door gently. Their home is dead quiet. He calms his breathing, locks the door, slips off his clothes and gets into bed. He tucks the eyeball under his mattress. Despite his excitement he is asleep in minutes. Exhaustion overtakes him.

Not long afterwards there is a thudding on the door.

He awakes with a start. At first he turns away, wraps the pillow over his head and tries to convince himself that he is dreaming. No one can be pounding on their door at this hour of the night.

But within seconds Wilber Holmes is on his feet and advancing toward the sound.

"Who's there?" he asks, his voice sounding shaky.

Sherlock will never forget the response.

"Police!" comes a thundering voice. "Open up!"

His father's answer is almost pleading.

"What do you want with us?"

"Open up or we will knock it down, sir!"

Wilber lets them in.

A plainclothes detective and two burly constables step heavily into the room. They have solemn looks on their faces, the policemen in helmets with black straps across their chins, long blue overcoats with wide belts around the middle, and thick black boots on their feet. One holds a "bull's eye" gas lantern in his hand.

"My name is Inspector Lestrade," states the man in the civilian clothes. He is an aging chap, perhaps nearly sixty, with a bushy mustache, and dressed in brown corduroy trousers, black waistcoat with a pocket watch on a chain, and dark brown coat; he is lean and ferret-like, but with a bulldog attitude. "Do you have a son?" he inquires.

"Why . . . why, yes."

"We need to speak with him."

Wilber turns and looks across the room at the little bed, terrified. He sees his son, sitting up, staring back at the police. There is a curious hardness in the boy's face, a look of steel in his gray eyes.

The three men advance across the room and surround him, as if he might try to escape.

"What's your name?"

"Sherlock Holmes."

"Were you, or were you not at the location of the Whitechapel murder past midnight this day?"

The boy pauses.

"I was."

Wilber is astonished.

"Sherlock? No. No! He couldn't have been. He was right here. He and his mother went to the opera."

"The opera?" inquires Lestrade, looking around at the poverty-stricken room. "Your wife attends the *opera*?"

"Jews," murmurs one constable to the other.

"We didn't actually attend," says the boy in an even voice. "We just stood outside and listened."

"Yes," says Wilber, "Yes, that's right. I misspoke myself."

"Indeed," responds Lestrade.

He eyes the boy again.

"You have been observed at the murder scene *twice*, on two consecutive days. What is your explanation?"

Wilbur is stunned. He tries to speak, but can't.

"I have none," says Sherlock.

"I see," snaps Lestrade. "You were also observed, by this constable," he motions to one of the policemen, "at the arraignment of Mohammad Adalji, the villain in this hideous affair. Not only were you observed there, but the accused spoke to you: only you. Did he not? Don't deny it."

"I won't."

Wilberforce Holmes stares, openmouthed, at his son.

"What did the Arab say?" Lestrade is twirling an end of his mustache.

"He said he didn't do it."

One of the constables barely hides a smirk.

"There is no question that he did it!" shouts Lestrade. "Are you involved with him?"

"No."

The inspector studies the boy's face for a while before he speaks again.

"Do you know something about this? Do you know something that we should know?"

Sherlock hesitates. He doesn't want to withhold evidence from the police, but he can't tell them about the glass eye, either. It might be the Arab's only chance, the only clue to what really happened. He can't just give it away, not to the very people who hold Adalji's life in their hands.

"No, sir."

"I'll ask you again."

"No need."

"Why?" The detective thinks the boy may be ready to confess something.

"I know nothing."

Lestrade's face turns red.

"We have jailed one scoundrel, young sir. But a coin purse is missing. We know that because we found beadwork particular to such an item in the alley. We know you frequent the streets, consort with gangs."

"My son does not con . . . " starts Wilber, but Sherlock cuts him off.

"I know nothing about the purse."

"Then you had better come with me," barks Lestrade.

"WHERE?"

It is Rose. She has risen from her bed and entered the room to see two policemen and an inspector surrounding her son.

"We are arresting your boy on suspicion of withholding evidence."

"Or on the possible involvement in a murder." It is the constable with the gas lantern. He looks at Mrs. Holmes with cold eyes. He is a soldier against evil and it shows.

"But that's absurd!" sputters Wilber Holmes and reaches out toward his son.

"Obstruct us and you will come too," says the constable.

The detective nods at the boy. The policemen seize him. Rose Holmes cries out. She tries to pull her son away, but Wilber takes her into his arms and holds her tightly. She beats her hands on his chest and then buries her face in his neck and sobs.

"Come quietly and there will be no difficulties," intones Lestrade. "We don't wish to cause anyone pain, but we must get to the bottom of this."

Sherlock goes quietly, indeed. In fact, he banishes his mother's cries and his father's eyes from his mind; erases them. He can't break down. Emotion won't get him anywhere. He must be like steel. As of this second, he *has* to find a solution to this crime. It isn't just the Arab who is in danger anymore.

Now . . . he has to save himself.

7

MOHAMMAD'S STORY

In the morning he awakes to a prayer, uttered in a weeping voice, soft and frightened. He starts upright on his stone bed, shocked to find himself in a dark little holding cell in the Bow Street Police Station.

He had dreamt of eyes. Thousands of eyes had been in his bed at home staring at him, pleading for help. A bigger one had emerged from under his mattress. All the others had turned to it.

That was what had first roused him. Then, as his head cleared, he heard the prayer. He once came across it in a book about the Crusades and remembers it well: he can photograph things with his mind's eye.

He swings his legs around and sits on the edge of the bed, listening. It is a call to Allah in a time of distress. Sound travels poorly in these cave-like rooms, but he can tell that the voice is coming from the cell next to his.

When it fades into silence, Sherlock sits, listening to his own breathing. Then he takes a chance.

"Mohammad?"

There is absolute stillness. Sherlock doesn't breathe. No answer.

He sighs and stands up. The hard bed is the only piece of furniture in the damp, stone room. There are no windows, just a small square opening with three bars cut at the height of his eyes in the big iron door. There is no mirror either, which irritates the boy: his hair must be terribly messy.

Suddenly, a sound ends the silence.

"Yes?" The voice is clear and quiet.

Sherlock advances to the door. Peering out, he sees the high wall of a long stone hallway and two small, barred windows on it, up very high. Twisting his neck and looking to the right, he can just see the fingers of two brown hands clutching the bars in the door next to his.

"Are you Mohammad Adalji?"

"Yes. But I didn't do it." He sounds firm and earnest. There is a slight eastern accent to his words.

"I'm the boy you spoke to outside the courthouse."

"You are?" A little hope creeps into Mohammad's voice.

"My name is Holmes."

"And you are in jail?"

Sherlock looks out the two small windows in the hallway where light is coming in. Finally, there is blue sky in London . . . and he's in here.

"They think I know something . . . that I'm connected to the murder in some way."

Mohammad says nothing for a moment and then speaks softly.

"I will tell them you were not involved."

"Much obliged, but they won't believe you."

"Yes they will, because they want to think I acted alone. I am an Arab."

"And I'm a Jew, a poor one."

"A Jew?" There is hesitation in the accused man's voice.

"Lower half Jewish, upper half English . . . respected part disowned."

"That is not good."

"Precisely."

Sherlock can hear the Arab sigh.

"Why do they suspect you?" he asks.

"Because you spoke to me."

Sherlock hears another sigh.

"I am sorry."

"And because I've been to the murder site . . . twice."

"You have?"

"I followed the crows." Sherlock pushes his face up tightly against the bars, trying to see more of his jailmate.

"Crows?"

"They landed right in the alley," muses the boy, seeing the scene again.

"They're . . . " murmurs the other, "they're *omens*. I saw some circling above the Old Bailey."

Sherlock is still remembering that last frightening trip to Whitechapel. "I went back a second time . . . because I pieced something together."

"What do you mean?" A tiny tone of hope returns to Mohammad's voice.

Sherlock doesn't answer at first. But if his listener could have seen him, he would have noticed a pleased expression beginning to spread across his face.

"Say that again," Sherlock demands.

"I merely asked a question."

"No, before that, about the crows."

"That I saw them." It had seemed like an innocent remark.

"And you said where?"

"Above the Old Bailey."

There is a long pause.

"Mr. Adalji, I don't think you committed the murder. I believe you." Sherlock's voice is matter-of-fact.

There is a short burst of laughter. "You are a strange young man, Master Holmes."

"I know."

"You will have to explain."

"Not until you do."

They stand shoulder to shoulder on either side of the wall, looking at each other's hands gripping the bars: dark ones and pale ones.

"I will tell anyone who will listen, Master Holmes."

"I am listening," responds Sherlock.

The brown hands tighten on the bars.

"I am a butcher's apprentice. I came to England from Egypt with my parents when I was eight . . . for a better life. I am good with a knife."

Sherlock gulps.

"But I use it just to slice and carve the meat. My boss is Muslim too, of course, and we work only with blessed, Halal cuts. He makes me work late into the night, and on the evening when the lady was killed, I had a delivery just after sunset. It was to a soup kitchen near where she was attacked. I push a heavy cart with big wooden wheels and it's difficult to turn sharply sometimes. I tried a shorter route on my return and went down the wrong street. It's easy to do in Whitechapel when night falls. I realized it halfway. So I turned around in that alley . . . the one where it happened. I had trouble with it, had to nose the cart back and forth several times. I remember I was in a rush. I built up a sweat, and then went as hard as I could go back home.

"Part of my job is cleaning up afterwards, after the butcher and the others are gone. He's a taskmaster, he is. I'm often there past midnight. That night was no exception, and as I was cleaning everything up, I came to the knives. I always do them last. Well . . . one knife, the big one . . . *it wasn't there.*"

Sherlock feels a shiver.

"I looked high and low, but it was nowhere to be seen. I wondered if I had mistakenly taken it with me on my delivery. So, I started retracing my steps in my head. There was only one place where I had done anything unusual: I'd turned around in tight quarters in that alley. It wasn't far from the shop.

I ran out into the darkness. There are some strange folk out of doors at night in London, Master Holmes. I ran with all I had to the alley. It was pitch black like a tunnel. It gave me the frights. I inched my way down there, feeling around with my boots, hoping to find the knife. Then . . . "

Mohammad's voice cracks. Next door the long, white fingers grip the bars.

"Then . . . I crouched down and felt around on the ground at about the spot where I figured I'd turned, where the knife was most apt to be. My hands were soon in a puddle . . . but it hadn't rained that night, Master Holmes. And the liquid . . . I thought it was water at first . . . was thick."

Mohammad pauses again.

"I felt her hair first . . . then her face . . . her open mouth. . . . I knew she was dead . . . I knew it was blood. . . . I stood up. And when I did, my shoe hit something. It clinked on the stones. I leaned over and felt for it. I knew what it was . . . *it was my knife.*"

Sherlock's eyes widen.

"I know now it was stupid, but I picked it up. I figured, I just figured that if anyone found my butcher's knife next to a dead woman . . . a knife belonging to an Arab . . . they'd hang me without asking one question. So I grabbed it and ran."

"Bloody footsteps all the way to the butcher's," says Sherlock without emotion.

"Yes. I was too scared to think straight. I just locked all the doors and slept in the little room the boss keeps for me, the knife in a rag under my coat, not thinking that I'd made a path to my door. The constables on the scene the next morning followed the trail right to me . . . and the knife."

Sherlock lets the story sink in. He is trying to fit it into what he knows.

"I didn't do it," repeats Mohammad, his voice cracking.

"I know."

"But you think I will hang."

"I didn't say that."

"But you *must* think it. How could anyone think anything else?" His despair is deepening. "There'll be no barrister to defend me. They have me! They have all the evidence and it is all against me. I have less than three weeks to live."

"I may have a clue," says the boy, lowering his voice as a jailer walks by. He pauses. "Something that may explain what really happened."

"In the name of Allah, tell me."

"Back home under the mattress on my bed . . . " Sherlock speaks under his breath again and looks around his cell as if worried that the very walls are listening, " . . . I have an eyeball."

"An eyeball?" asks Mohammad.

8

THE UNUSUAL GIRL

Sherlock won't say anything more. He doesn't think it wise. It is dawning on him that there is something suspicious about the fact that he's been placed in this cell right next to Mohammad Adalji. When he mentioned the eye he spoke quietly and cautioned his new friend to lower his voice and say nothing more.

The police are listening. He is sure. He hopes he hasn't said too much already. He examines his cell in more detail: there are tiny holes in the ceiling; little cracks in the wall; he is imprisoned near the door that leads right to the office.

The boy spends the day lying on his stone bed trying to understand his situation. It is difficult to concentrate. He is frightened. The Arab is indeed going to die. And here *he* is, helpless: associated with an open-and-shut murder case. What are they going to do to him? What *can* they do to someone held on suspicion of withholding evidence? They've imprisoned him, haven't they? And they aren't letting him go. But what if it's even worse? *What if they think he and Mohammad killed that woman together?* He feels his stomach burn.

Oh, God. As the day wears on, his spirit sinks as low as the new London sewers. The Arab's desperate prayers fill the cells.

Every time Sherlock thinks of his mother and father he looks to the door hoping to see them. He wants them here, to hug him and tell him it is all a dream. He thinks of how desperately upset they must be. But the jail begins to grow dark and they don't appear. It doesn't make sense. Why aren't they coming?

"Jailer!" he finally shouts, rising to his feet.

The stern-looking turnkey moves slowly toward him.

"Why aren't my mother and father . . . ?"

"Perhaps they're busy," the man growls.

It's obvious . . . his parents aren't *allowed* to visit. He explodes.

"You can't keep them from me! You can't keep me here!"

The jailer walks away.

Sherlock falls onto the bed, shaking. *Control yourself,* he thinks. He must reason this through. *Do they really believe we killed her together?* He slows his breathing. They charged Mohammad with murder, not him. Why are they trying to break him down and why spy on him? Don't they already have what they need to hang Adalji?

And then it dawns on him. He puts the facts together . . . how the police are treating him, their focus on the purse when they questioned him, all of it. Everything becomes clear.

He mumbles to himself as he lies on the bed, knees drawn to his chest.

"They think they know *exactly* what happened."

He can see it now.

"I wasn't *really* arrested for withholding evidence. I'm not being held in jail for that, or for murder. They think I'm guilty of something else."

He knows their theory.

"We're thieves and work together. . . . The Arab is bigger and good with a knife, he was simply meant to scare her with it . . . I was young, fast, and street-wise, meant to snatch the treasure and make off with it . . . the Jew's job. But our robbery went badly. She struggled and the Arab killed her. I fled with the purse. I hid it somewhere in a hurry and I keep going back to the area to get it, but haven't retrieved it yet. *That's* what they think! That's why they're holding me in jail without visitors and why they placed us beside each other. They want to see if I'll let something slip about the purse to Mohammad, or better still, confess. . . . Then they will have the Arab, the half-breed, *and* the money."

Strangely, for an instant this discovery actually makes him feel a little better. Now he has two clues: the glass eye and an understanding of the authorities' motives. He isn't entirely helpless anymore. He has lit a small candle, however dim, at the entrance to the tunnel of this mystery.

But what consolation is that? Doesn't this mean they think Sherlock an accessory to murder? Can't they put him *to death* for it? He won't have a barrister, either. They can *hang boys at thirteen!* He curls up into a ball on the bed, petrified. What hope does he have now? Nothing can ever give him hope again.

But he is wrong. The very next day, hope comes into the jail in the form of a girl.

She arrives about noon, accompanied by her father.

A turnkey and a constable strut up to Mohammad's cell. They take him out. The constable holds a pistol cocked and pointed; the turnkey binds the prisoner's hands behind his back and shoves him onto a chair. There, his feet are strapped to the wooden legs. They push him, chair and all, back into his cell.

"Mr. Andrew C. Doyle," bellows the jailer, "and his daughter, Irene, with express permission of Scotland Yard."

The large man with the big walrus mustache and well- cut tweed suit doesn't interest Sherlock. The girl doesn't either, at first. They pass him. The man's eyes, brimming with kindness, never stray from Mohammad in the next cell, but the girl notices Sherlock through his barred window. She glances his way: just a glance. There are questions in her face.

The boy goes back to his bed and sits on it, listening.

"Good day, Mr. Adalji, I am as announced," says the man in loud but friendly tones that are obviously meant to soothe. *Slight Scottish accent*, thinks the boy, *raised in the Edinburgh area, came to London in his teens, religious, a free-thinker, and a respected philanthropist.* Sherlock sizes him up in an instant. The boy is especially glad of his skill of analysis now. As of today, it will be very important to know others well and imagine what sort of threat they might be. He has made it a point to study traits such as accents, even how they fade after people settle in London. He can tell many things by the tone of the man's voice, the fact that he is in a jail speaking with a foreigner accused of murder, and his clothes. He is a spiritual man (though perhaps a dissenter), holds certain political views, wants to help others, gives to the poor.

"This is my daughter, Irene."

"Pleased to meet you, sir," she says kindly.

The boy imagines her sitting on the stone bed next to her well-groomed father, looking sympathetically into the eyes of the poor accused murderer. She'd floated past in an instant, but Sherlock recalls her perfectly.

"I am with The Society of the Visiting Friends of London," begins Mr. Doyle. "We comfort the unfortunate, the guilty, the falsely accused, whatever you are, sir. We go into the rookeries, the jails, and opium dens. I read about your case in *The Times* and was given special permission to see you. We are simply here to talk. We will not judge you. Everything said between us will stay between us."

"I didn't do it."

"That is between you and God. We are your friends."

The girl is tall for her age. Sherlock likes that. She has long blonde hair that curls at the top and runs down the back of her neck in thick, shining waves; and dark brown eyes, darker than his own gray ones. Her clothes are plain: a white blouse frilled a little near the neck where a red ribbon is tied, a beige woolen shawl, a dark cotton dress that hangs down almost to the top of her black boots, no crinoline. She seems about his age. He likes that too. He wonders what questions she had when she looked at him. And he wonders why she and her father don't judge Mohammad Adalji.

Sherlock wishes he could know more about her. But for some reason he can't get a complete picture. She is a bit of a mystery. He likes that too.

The Arab won't say much to the Doyles. He speaks a little about his past, about coming to England, his dreams. But he always stops before he arrives at that horrible night in the East End. Sherlock can hear the girl responding to him, encouraging him to say more. But before long, he simply stops.

They thank him and call for a turnkey. Then they stand outside the cell while Mohammad is untied. Mr. Doyle blesses him with a Christian prayer. As he does, Sherlock gets up and watches from his door. He has a clear view through the bars. Irene has her eyes closed, her hands clasped in front of her. Sherlock lowers his head. When he lifts it, she is looking at him.

The prayer finishes at that instant. She closes her eyelids abruptly and then opens them again. Andrew Doyle regards Sherlock.

"Bless you, my son," he says.

Irene simply nods.

And then they are gone.

It has a remarkable effect on Sherlock. A sort of peace comes over him. The cells seem even dimmer without her. He thinks long and hard about those dark brown eyes.

In the night, he tries again to imagine more about her. But still, she seems elusive. He isn't used to that. He thinks of the advice his father so often gives him.

"Observation," Wilber always says, "is not only the primary skill of the scientist, it is the elementary talent of life. Use your eyes at all times, my boy. They will not lie to you if you focus them fully. Use all your senses: hearing, smelling, tasting, and touching (though that last one, your mother can say more about than I). Truly seeing things is a great power. It will give you strength even when fate seems to have made you weak."

But try as he might, he can't *truly* see this girl. He estimates her age, remembers her face, that hair, but that is all.

The next day, he lies in his cell feeling sorry for himself, convinced there is no way out of the hole he is in.

Then he hears a sweet voice.

"I understand your name is Sherlock Holmes."

He almost leaps to his feet. She has come alone this time. It has taken remarkable courage. Respectable young ladies rarely venture out alone in London.

"Yes," is all he can say. She is standing in the hall in front of a burly turnkey who clutches a truncheon in his hand.

"You are very young to be in jail, sir," she says.

"I am innocent."

He wishes he hadn't said the words the instant he utters them. He is sure that every prisoner who has ever been in this jail has said them many times. And he is very sure that she has heard them so often that it makes her numb.

"I am your friend," she responds.

Those words sound wonderful.

"They want me to talk with you from the hallway." She smiles. "And I don't want them to tie you up." The turnkey is walking away down the hall and she lowers her voice, "I'm surprised they allowed me in, though father's name carries a great deal of weight. I was passing the Opera House across the street in the crowds with my governess and slipped away. I have never done anything quite like this before, but you looked awfully lonely yesterday." She takes a breath. "Father has always taught me to be independent, you know, very much so. We do things differently at our house . . . though this may be a bit *too* different, even for him. Miss Stamford is likely quite frantic by now!"

They exchange smiles. Irene's nervous talkativeness makes Sherlock like her even more. She is wearing a red dress this time, dark red, and a crinoline underneath that makes it billow out, ending just above her white-stocking ankles. She holds a pretty blue shawl around her shoulders.

He stands at the steel door, his nose pressed through the bars. She smells like soap. The words pour out of him.

"I am here only because I read about the murder, because I visited the crime scene twice, because Mohammad spoke to me."

Her presence is doing something to him.

"I won't judge –"

"No . . . don't say that. I *really* didn't do anything wrong. But I'm going to do something now. It's time someone did. I'm going to solve this crime. And not just for me, or Mohammad. Whoever killed that poor woman needs to be brought to justice. . . . It isn't fair!" He pauses, realizing that he's almost shouted the last three words and they've echoed down the hallway.

It had been a waterfall of frantic words. Now there is silence. She simply looks at him, not sure what to say. She really shouldn't be here, but this unusual boy has drawn her.

"Solve it?" she asks.

"I have a clue," he says in a quiet voice.

The main door slams open. A man appears in the hallway: Inspector Lestrade. The ferret-like detective fixes his eyes on Sherlock's.

"Having a chat with Miss Doyle, are we? Anything you'd like to share?"

Sherlock is aghast at his slip. Maybe this is why they let her in. He'd actually mentioned the clue! Had he said it too loudly? He didn't think so. But the inspector knew he'd mentioned something important and had deemed a sudden confrontation worthwhile.

"Well?" asks Lestrade.

"I . . . I'm . . . just . . . " He looks at Irene. There aren't questions in her eyes anymore, just understanding. "I was . . . just . . . boasting, sir, to this young lady."

The inspector observes Irene, who gives him a shy smile. Then he stands still for a long time, staring at Sherlock. The boy drops his eyes. They can all hear the big clock in the office ticking through the main door. The inspector starts tapping his foot in time to it.

"We have some discussions in our future, you and I!" Then he vanishes almost as quickly as he appeared.

Irene comes back the next day. This time her governess is with her, waiting in the office, bearing a note from Mr. Doyle allowing her to visit when accompanied. Last night, after Miss Stamford made her distressing report, Irene had apologized to her father, but then asked if she might begin to do some of "their work." Mr. Doyle was impressed. (She had calculated that he would be.) He is raising her to be a strong, unique woman with a social conscience, and unusual, even unladylike ambition is to be encouraged. She didn't mention that the first place she wanted to visit was the Bow Street Police Station.

Inside the jail, their conversation grows. They talk about their lives. He is amazed by her bravery, but also her sense of duty, love for her father and his mission, her kindness, and intelligence. She finds herself revealing details she normally keeps from inmates, and even mentions the street where she lives. He, in turn, tells her marvelous things: he shows off.

"Our jailer is five feet seven and a half inches tall, calculated by the length of his stride in the hallway. He is left-handed, married with three children, two girls and a boy. And did I mention he is forty-six years, five months, and seventeen days old?"

"You are making that up, you rascal," she says, smiling.

"Partly," he admits. "I heard the other turnkey tease him about his age."

But the rest is true and he proves it. Then he does the trick again: about the other turnkey. It is like magic. It makes her laugh. But when he changes the subject and tells her about his life, he sees tears in her eyes. He is a loner, and desperate to be more than the world has allowed him to be.

But Sherlock Holmes isn't just talking. There is a method to his conversation.

He made up his mind the night before that there are two things he absolutely has to do: keep his mouth shut about what he knows . . . and get out of jail. Irene Doyle is his only connection to the outside. If he has any chance, it will have to be through her.

Slowly, without once saying anything directly about the crime or what he knows of it, he tries to show her that he is the sort of person who shouldn't be in jail. She's met many prisoners; he has to somehow convince her that he has been falsely accused. He speaks of his sense of justice, and subtly hints with expressions in his eyes that he knows something about the murder: something that might free him, and Mohammad too. All he needs is a chance.

The next morning, as he takes his breakfast of glue-like porridge, hoping Irene will visit again, his mind is racing. His eyes dart around his cell and up and down the hall for any way out. But escape from the Bow Street jail seems impossible. It is sealed like a canning jar. He thinks until his mind goes in circles. Finally he stands up and jams his wooden spoon into the goop in the bowl. He starts to pace. *Nothing!* Nothing will work. When he finally sits down, he notices something peculiar. The spoon is still sticking straight up in the porridge. It hasn't moved an inch. And when he tries to pull it out, it takes some effort. He taps the food with his hand. It has hardened into a remarkably solid mass. He can see the perfectly shaped outline of the business end of his spoon in the stiff mound. His heart beats faster. He wedges out a small piece of porridge and slips it into his pocket, then returns the bowl to the turnkey. A few hours later, when Irene comes through the door as fresh as an English country breeze, the chunk of porridge feels as hard as stone.

He molds their conversation again, trying to pull all the right levers, and just before she leaves, he makes a pointed comment.

"You wouldn't want to eat the porridge in these parts," he remarks with a smile, but looks straight into her eyes as if he is entering them. "It not only tastes like Plaster of Paris, but if you let it sit for a while, it *hardens* like it too.

I would be willing to wager that I could make a *tool* out of it . . . that would split wood."

Her eyes widen. She thinks for a moment, as if trying to make a decision. Without saying another word, she rises and leaves the jail.

There *is* a way out of this cell. And indeed . . . Irene Doyle is the key.

ESCAPE

The Bow Street jail serves breakfast to its inmates at six o'clock in the morning. At exactly that time two days later, before natural light has even illuminated the street, Irene Doyle appears at the front desk asking to see Sherlock Holmes. It is a strange request, especially given that her governess is nowhere in sight. The clerk sergeant on duty hesitates, but he knows the Doyles and their eccentric ways, and assumes that Irene has a good reason – a humane reason – to be here at this hour. Perhaps the accused boy is particularly lonely in the morning. He assumes a hansom cab awaits her.

But Irene Doyle has come alone, sneaking from her bed in the early hours and racing through the awakening streets, petrified, her shawl pulled up over her face. Before she met Sherlock, she wouldn't have imagined doing what she is about to do. Perhaps it is evil. Or is it in the service of justice? She has decided to take a chance.

There are five Bobbies on morning duty: the sergeant at his large wooden desk in the reception area behind the public waiting room at the front entrance, an assistant at a smaller desk to his left, two constables on guard inside the main doors, and a turnkey attending to the prisoners in the holding cells.

Irene arrives just in time. The heavily whiskered jailer is emerging from the kitchen below stairs, his big black boots pounding up the worn, old wooden steps, seven bowls of porridge and seven tin cups of tea balanced on a wooden tray. His keys dangle from a ring on his belt.

"May I come with you?" she asks, as she hastily signs the visitors' book.

"Uh . . . " the turnkey looks at his superior. The clerk sergeant nods.

"Right this way, Miss."

They walk past the desks toward a big, iron door at the back of the reception room. A constable meets them there. He opens the door, ushers them through, and follows. The cells are down five stone steps at the back of the station house, on ground level, in long whitewashed hallways gathered around a central courtyard.

Sherlock doesn't register any surprise when he sees Irene appear with the two men.

Today, all the prisoners confined in the holding area are in one hallway. The jailer will start distributing the gooey paste at the far end of the passage, working his way back to the boy, who is nearest the entrance.

Irene stops at Sherlock's cell. She nods to him. They begin talking about the weather as the policemen walk away down the hall to give out the porridge.

Soon the two Peelers return. There is just one bowl left. The jailer stands in front of Sherlock's cell, the constable

looking on as he searches for the right key, a big, uncompli-
cated iron instrument. He finds it and inserts it into the lock.

"May I serve him?" Irene says.

It is another strange request and it makes the turnkey
uncomfortable. He has a routine. He likes routines. He
glances at the constable and then back at Irene.

"Uh . . . I'm, uh . . . "

Irene takes the bowl from the tray. The big key is still
in the lock. In order to hand the bowl to Sherlock, she has to
step between the jailer and the key, which is attached to the
man's belt by a small chain. She reaches out and pulls the key
from the lock. As she does, she drops it into the bowl.

"Oh my!" she cries.

"Not a worry, Miss," says the jailer, gingerly remov-
ing the iron tool from the porridge. "He'll eat it no matter
what. That's all they get 'til past noon." He places a
beefy arm in front of her. "But I'm afraid I have to serve
him. Regulations."

Irene hands over the porridge and stands back. The
turnkey opens the door and passes the bowl to Sherlock,
who takes it and sets it on his stone bed. He looks down
at it. The distinct outline of the key remains clear on the
surface of the thick porridge, next to the wooden spoon that
stands almost straight up.

Sherlock leaves it standing. He can hear the door close
behind him.

"Aren't you going to eat, Holmes?" asks the turnkey,
peering through the bars.

"I'm not very hungry."

The big jailer laughs. "You will be. Inspector Lestrade has scheduled a . . . 'discussion' . . . with you for tomorrow morning. I'd suggest you eat up."

But Sherlock doesn't move.

"Suit yourself."

The jailer shrugs. He has a chair in a spot where he can see all the prisoners' doors, but he likes to pace back and forth. Each morning since Sherlock has been there, the guard has paced seven times up and down the hallway before he sits. On his fifth trip this morning, Irene intercepts him. They meet at a point where he can't see inside Holmes' cell and she delays him, inquiring about the details of visiting hours this week.

The instant she departs to meet the jailer, Sherlock rushes across the cell to his bed. He takes out the wooden spoon, scoops off the surface of the porridge and sets the layer of hardening paste, complete with the key's impression, on the bed against the wall, then dips out another blob, this one much bigger, and plops it down beside the other. When he is done, he sits in front of them.

Irene thanks the turnkey for the information and lets him return to his routine. She quickly says good-bye to Sherlock, walks up the steps toward the front office, and the big door opens and closes. The turnkey's footsteps echo down the hallway, getting nearer.

"Ah, I see you have regained your appetite, Master Holmes." Sherlock is seated on his bed, the bowl of porridge on his knees, spoon in hand, apparently partway through his meal.

Every time the jailer rises to pace that morning, Sherlock turns like a cat to his two splats of porridge next to the wall. Within half an hour, he has made his very own porridge key. He finishes just in time. The paste has almost hardened into its infamous rock-like consistency.

\

The Bow Street jailers are certainly not supposed to sleep on duty. But Sherlock knows they sometimes do. Frightened and unable to settle in, he has awakened several times the last few nights, and each time has made an observation: his night watchman, sitting on the chair down the hall, has a habit of nodding off at about four o'clock in the morning. The boy knows the hour by the position of the moon, which he can see through one of the little hall windows, that looks out into the courtyard.

He watches the moon through his bars. The crude key, modeled on an equally crude one that is meant for a very roomy lock, is clutched in his hand. It is as hard as a cricket bat.

Sure enough, at about four o'clock, the jailer's chin goes down onto his chest. He is a veteran who can likely rouse himself from slumber at the scratch of a rat.

Sherlock inserts the key.

He tries to turn it. The lock creaks. The turnkey stirs.

"Prudence, I drank but one mug of beer, I swear . . . " he mutters, never opening his eyes, his mouth munching as if he were tasting something. He drifts off again.

The boy is frozen in place beside the keyhole. He waits. But not too long: the jailers' naps are always short.

The key is still in the lock. He tries to turn it. It won't budge. Maybe his key isn't sturdy enough. He tries again. This time he holds it directly in the center of the lock so it will push the bolt perfectly and turns it very slowly, praying it won't snap. But he can feel his porridge-iron tool beginning to crack. He pulls it out and tries one more time, twisting even more gingerly. Slowly . . . it turns.

He's unlocked the cell!

Now he has to open the door. It squeaks every time the jailers move it.

Sherlock begins pushing the door gently. Every few seconds it creaks and the turnkey stirs, but soon he's opened it enough to slip out. He slides into the hallway. He can't believe it. His heart is pounding. He moves toward the main door, but then stops.

Mohammad.

When he sneaks to the next cell, he is shocked to see the Arab looking back at him, wide awake, standing right at the bars. There is a different look in the man's eyes in the darkness. They appear calculating. The accused man doesn't seem so young anymore.

The jailer stirs again.

The two prisoners stare at each other for several breaths. How does Sherlock know for *sure* that Mohammad Adalji is telling the truth? He is almost certain, but not absolutely. Not yet. He turns . . . and tiptoes away. The Arab nearly reaches out to grab him. For an instant, it seems like he might shout. But he holds himself back, anger burning in his face.

In a heartbeat, silent as a ghost, Sherlock moves up the steps, through the door at the end of the hallway, barely opens it, and slides through. He finds himself in the reception room of the front office. Looking ahead and to his right he sees a small desk and then a large, wooden one farther away. No one is at the first, but a night sergeant sits at the second. Sherlock is slightly behind him. The man's head is down. He's writing in his books, dipping his pen in an ink bottle. The boy drops to the floor and advances to the smaller desk, crouching behind it, out of sight. His breathing sounds as loud to him as the bellows the old hatter uses when he lights his fireplace. He tries to calm himself. The policeman is five yards away. Sherlock starts sorting through the photographs his mind took of the front part of the Bow Street Divisional Police Station when he was brought in a week ago. He knows that the London evening and freedom are to his left, through an open archway in this room, and then about six steps across the waiting room and out the big, black front doors. But the night sergeant, whom he can't entirely see, can spot anyone who goes in or out.

He peeks around the desk and looks through the archway where he spies a Bobbie sitting on one of the benches in the front room.

He'll have to make a run for it. But the element of surprise will be in his favor. He'll use his street smarts and get past the sergeant in a flash. There is really only one policeman to elude. When he gets to the other room, he will know exactly where to find the front doors and their latch.

Then a noise comes from behind.

"What in the name of –" a voice exclaims. It is the old jailer, who has roused from his sleep to find an empty cell.

Sherlock leaps to his feet.

Run!

He makes for the open archway, the jailer in hot pursuit, darting through the room in an instant. He figures the Bobbie on the bench in the outer room will rise to stop him, so he goes low, like a rugby athlete below a scrum. Down he goes, under the Peeler's grasp and out into that waiting room. *There are the doors.* But suddenly policemen are materializing out of walls! Three more Bobbies are on their feet – all had been lounging on other benches, hidden from his view.

But he was right: he has the element of surprise. Speed is what matters. Only one policeman, close to the doors, has a chance to collar him. The man dives at him. He ducks again and the Bobbie flies over him, catching part of his black frock coat in a hand. The boy wrenches himself free and flings a big door open. In a second he is fleeing down the stone steps, past the wrought-iron gates and round blue lamps, and into the night.

That strangeness is in the streets again: that eerie opera of bizarre people and criminals who come out in the dark. Sherlock races through this nightmare, the Force on his trail. He hears the violins again, playing frantically. The fog hangs thick tonight.

The last thing he did as he lay awake in the dark was make a plan for what he would do if he made it outside. He thought of every possible situation, all the way from the best . . . to the one he is in now, with Bobbies in close pursuit. He can't go home; he can't outrun the police; he can't hide for long because no one will hide him . . . except maybe a criminal, one who lives on the streets, who knows how to avoid the authorities, who might in some twisted way, feel there is something to gain by helping him.

Malefactor! Where are you?

He races across Bow Street, west into Covent Garden, running past the gas-lit Opera House without even giving it a glance. He never won a single race in school, but that was because he hadn't cared. When he cares, he can do nearly anything. His legs are thin and long like a greyhound's.

He turns north and up toward the narrower streets, places he knows Malefactor frequents with his Irregulars. His boots hammer on the cobblestones. Rain drizzles down again. He hears the sound of his own explosive breathing.

Where are they?

He has no good reason to believe that the boy criminal will help him. It's just a feeling, an intuition of the sort that he often has about that nefarious street knave: that something about this situation will appeal to him, that he and Malefactor have some indefinable attachment. His enemy may just save him in order to hound him.

They often stay near here. Somewhere.

As he flies, he glances down every alleyway. Nothing. The police are shouting behind him, their voices echoing in the dim, fog-filled streets. He scrambles west, past closed taverns and black shop windows, and then up a narrow street to the north. In seconds it becomes even narrower. Then he realizes where he is . . . *in The Seven Dials*. He has never dared to come here before, to this intersection of seven little streets in the heart of London: an infamous part of the rotting core, known for its abject poverty, its violence – and as a haunt of thieves. But this is where he has to be. This is where Malefactor can be found.

The police are getting closer, their boots pounding louder in pursuit. At the intersection, he selects a street and runs into that dark artery. It is a canyon of broken-down three-storey buildings. Several half-clothed people lie on the narrow foot pavements and out onto the road. He flashes past tight little passageways jutting off from the street, where only the human sewer rats of London go. Skidding past one, he notices some movement in the darkness.

Irregulars?

It would make sense. The little alley bulges out into a tiny court and then narrows again on the other side. It is a perfect place for them to sleep. He vanishes into the passage, heading for the shadows. Even now, in his desperate situation, this frightens him to his boots. He's never slithered into a hole like this.

A human head is slowly lifting and facing him through the fog. Then a whole torso rises. Sherlock comes to a sudden halt. There are bodies lying everywhere. The torso is long and thin.

"Master Holmes, I perceive."

He doesn't even sound sleepy. All around their leader, the Irregulars are lying in heaps, snoring loudly.

"Malefactor!"

"Troubles, young sir?" His yellowing teeth are dimly evident in the dark. He looks pleased.

"They're after me."

"Heard you'd been for a visit at the Bow. Escaped have we?"

There is a tinge of admiration in his voice.

"*They're after me!*"

Malefactor glances down the passageway behind Sherlock. The first policeman has arrived. He is peering in, hesitating despite the nearness of his prey.

"This way!" exclaims Malefactor, shoving Sherlock past him. "Go east, then north. Vanish!"

Sherlock doesn't need to hear more. He struggles to pass Malefactor, stepping on Irregulars. They groan and swear and begin to rise.

"Let him through!" hisses their boss. "I'll expect a report! Some information!"

Sherlock is gone, out the other end of the alley. Malefactor turns to face the policemen coming their way.

"Irregulars! Stand up and stay standing! I want a delay of at least a minute for Master Holmes this evening. These crushers have nothing on us, can't nick us for standing in a walkway."

The police collide with the Irregulars. Heated curses come from the deeper voices, earnest apologies from the younger. But somehow, despite apparent attempts on the part of the Irregulars to get out of the way, they seem to keep placing themselves directly in front of the Bobbies. It is nearly a minute before they get to the end of the passage. When they look out onto the street beyond, the boy has vanished.

His father has taught him to listen to experts, so he does as Malefactor says. If the boy criminal says to go east then north, then east and north he will go. There's another reason, a very good one, to flee in that direction.

He zigzags as he flies, until he reaches the trees on beautiful Bloomsbury Square. He's entering an area where the police would not expect him to be. The British Museum, that wonderful depository of information, is down the street to his left; farther ahead stands the University College of London, where his father's dreams once seemed possible.

He is nearly out of breath. He hasn't heard or seen the Bobbies for several minutes. It is time to walk. He won't look as suspicious this way either.

This is a very different neighborhood from his own. It's where the educated reside: professors, philanthropists, and where he can find . . . Irene.

Yes. North and east has been the perfect direction, fitting into the last part of his escape plan.

Irene and her father live *somewhere* near here. Montague Street: that's what she said. The avenue he is now on is well lit with tall, black iron gas lamps – all the wealthy areas are. He walks north to the end of the foot pavement and looks up at the name imprinted on the last building. Bedford Place. He is close; he knows it. He is at the south end of another park. He turns left toward the Museum, massive and made of gray stone with Roman pillars, rising on the west side of . . . Montague.

Irene is asleep somewhere on this street.

He prowls along the footpath, examining the houses. They are all in a row, all attached, narrow, but three-and-a-half storeys high, with cream-colored ground floors and brown brick or white stone on the upper levels. Bright flowers grow in window boxes. Numbers aren't posted on all the houses, but some have business and family names.

He keeps reading, squinting from the street, not daring to go close to the front doors. Shiny, black iron fences guard each residence; a few stone steps lead up to the entrances, servants' quarters are below. When he is all the way down the street, across from the Museum, he stops near a brick home. It has a brass plaque. He squints: "Society . . . of . . . Visiting . . . Friends. . . ."

He's found her.

But now what? He can't just walk up the steps and knock. Mr. Doyle would immediately return him to jail.

He looks in both directions. No one is on the street. The Doyles' house is attached to the dwelling to its north, but it is at the end of the row where a little passage about two feet wide cuts through to the back of the property. An iron gate stretches across it. He crouches down and moves toward it. The gate opens easily. He inches along the passage and soon finds himself next to a walled backyard the width of the house and about eight feet long. Through an entrance in the wall he can see that a good part of the small yard is filled with a little house . . . made for a dog.

Oh-oh!

Frantic, he returns to the passage. He faces the yard as he moves backward, ready for an attack or furious barking. But there is nothing. That is curious. The dog hasn't noticed him. Could it be asleep? Is it ancient and hard of hearing? He spots its chain, lying on the bricks on the ground, and stops. It isn't attached to anything.

A minute later he is lying in the empty dog kennel. Whatever canine the Doyles may own isn't occupying its little mansion just now. Sherlock curls up, reluctantly wraps a stinking blanket around his legs, and sets his head on the hard ground, his eyes wide and his heart still thumping. When he finally settles, his first thoughts are of his mother. He needs to see his parents. He feels like he's been running for days. Tears well up in his eyes. He stops them. *Drift off,* he tells himself, *drift off. There's much to do. There's much to prove.*

Not long afterwards, he is fast asleep.

10

IN DISGUISE

He doesn't wake until the sun is well up in the sky. And even then, it takes him a while to rouse himself. Feeling cold and sore, he slowly raises his head, instinctively fixes his hair, and then looks down his grimy clothing toward his boots and out the open kennel door.

Two eyes are staring back at him!

He tries to stand and smacks his head against the roof.

"Sherlock!"

Irene.

"You made it? You came *here*? To *my* house?" She speaks as if she were looking at an apparition.

But it is the ghost himself who is most frightened.

"H-How did you know I was in here?" He asks, his voice shaking. "Is there anyone else at home?" His eyes dart past the edge of the door, surveying the backyard, glancing up at the windows on every floor.

"No. Father's gone out and we don't keep servants in the house. He doesn't believe in it. We do many of the chores. He pays a maid-of-all-works to help a few hours every day. She's already been and gone, and my governess

is off today. I looked out here and saw a boot sticking out."
She pauses, staring at him. "I helped you escape from a jail!"
For an instant it looks like she might get up and run. "You
have to promise me something. You have to promise that
you are . . . " She is flustered and pauses again, " . . . good."
Then she seems uncomfortable. "I didn't express that well.
What I mean is . . . "

"I *am* good," he says, looking at her intently. "I
promise. I'm not a criminal, Irene."

"But you can't stay here. Can you?"

"I can if you help me."

"Well . . . you'll need food . . . and dry clothes."

Normally Sherlock would be upset about the state of
his garments. But for once their condition isn't important.

"We need to know what *really* happened to that
woman."

"We do? You . . . and me?"

"Otherwise I'm in deep trouble . . . and Mohammad
will die. He barely has two weeks left."

She thinks for a second.

"Come into the house."

Sherlock meets the dog just inside the back door.

The one and only John Stuart Mill.

He is a squat little brown-and-white Corgi who is past
middle-age, with short, stubby legs, ridiculously tall ears,
and is thick, both around his middle and between those

startling hearing apparatus. He also has an evident problem with gas. The instant Sherlock enters the house, the slow-moving, slow-thinking little beast exerts an embarrassing noise from one end of his plump body and seizes the bottom of one of the boy's trouser legs with the other, clamping on with a ferocious grip and not letting go.

"J.S. Mill is very protective," says Irene with a red face, tugging him away from her friend. "I'll put him downstairs. He has the run of the house as long as he behaves. . . . He decided he didn't like sleeping outdoors some time ago."

Their home is all wood and warmth. Huge colorful rugs lie on the floors, expensive paintings cover nearly every inch of the walls, and French furniture fills the many rooms. She marches Sherlock upstairs from the ground level, past the drawing room on the first floor, to the second, turns him down the hallway past her father's bedroom, and then to her own. She closes the door from the outside. With her voice fading as she tiptoes away, she asks him to take off his clothes and drop them in the hall. He does and a minute later hears her walk gingerly back down the shining wood floor to retrieve them.

"Stay in there," she calls, sounding nervous, almost commanding him. She is alone in the house with a boy. "I'll have them clean and dry in two hours. There are towels by my washstand." He hears her descending several flights, all the way down into the below-stairs area to where the servants and a laundress would normally work. Irene Doyle is indeed unusual.

There he is, in her room. It is a bit like being in heaven. He is distant from the depths of Southwark, the hell of his own home. He pours some water from a china pitcher into a basin on her washstand, finds some soap nearby, and washes himself, relieved to finally be clean. He pats his straight, black hair into place in a mirror and then looks around. Everything is bright; everything smells good. There are photographs on her dressing table and all over her walls. It looks like a gallery. Famous people are posed. He recognizes Adelina Patti, the great singer, the one and only "Champagne Charlie," Leotard, the "Daring Young Man on the Flying Trapeze," and many others. Her frilly red bed is stacked with sand-stuffed cloth animals. Books fill shelves. He sits on the floor and picks out a few. There's Dickens of course, Thackeray, Wilkie Collins, Austen, and Poe, and some remarkably thick ones about Far Eastern history and English social issues, most in three-volume sets. He's had no books, magazines, or even papers in jail. It has been a week since he's read a single word on a printed page. Reading is like an addiction to him: he craves it the way desperate folks in the Lime House opium dens in the East End need their drug. He eyes the volumes hungrily. But it's the children's books that he can't put down. He sits for a long time turning their pages, smiling at the ones whose insides pop up. It seems like only moments later that a rap comes on the door and a slim arm enters like a snake being charmed, and drops his clean clothes on the floor.

"Put them on," she says. He hears her footsteps fleeing along the hallway and then down the stairs.

A short while later, they sit at the gleaming dining table on the ground floor, he in his worn but clean dark suit, she in another immaculate dress, this time partially covered by an apron. In front of him is a banquet of food – crumpets and tea, kippers and orange juice, links and eggs, the sort of food he's rarely tasted. A yellow lark sits in a gold cage hanging from the ceiling almost over their shoulders, hopping from its perch onto a little green square of sod and back, fluttering its wings as if looking for a way out. It doesn't say anything. Neither does Sherlock, who eats like a starving man. He speaks only when he's finished every last morsel, and then his voice is shaking with emotion.

"I need to know how my parents are and get word to them . . . that I'm alive."

But he knows a visit would be reckless, almost impossible.

"I have to see Malefactor first," he adds.

"Who?"

"He's a boy who lives on the streets and operates a gang. He hates me. But I have the feeling he'll help me now, show me how to survive, do what I have to do. I have information I can trade, tell him things about the Bow Street jail, about how . . . "

Sherlock springs to his feet and heads for the front door.

"Stop!" shouts Irene.

The boy turns.

"Two things: you can't go out in broad daylight, they are looking for you; and, when you do go, I'm coming with you."

Her first point makes perfect sense. He feels like a fool for being so rash. The second part stuns him. Certainly, he had hoped she would help him: bring him food, let him stay near the house, not give him up to the police. But come with him to visit the Irregulars? He doesn't care how unusual she is – he has no intention of bringing her with him.

"Right," he says, "on both counts."

Mr. Doyle is supposed to be away for most of the day, so Sherlock is able to stay indoors for a while longer. The boy is well aware that it is improper for them to be alone together, but they have little choice. With time to themselves, they talk, each vigilant for any noise at the front door.

"My father is a man of some means, but not like most who have money," she tells Sherlock with pride, motioning for him to clear the plates off the table and help her take them down to the kitchen.

Andrew Doyle, it turns out, is an Oxford-educated scion of a liberal family who can afford to spend his days at the head of an organization that not only aids the poor, but tries to make the government help them too. He is willing to leave the comfort of his home to roll up his sleeves and contribute in the hospitals, the jails, and even on the streets. He is a "new thinker" of the 1860s, gone from nearly sunrise to sunset, attempting to change the world.

"He wasn't always that way," says Irene, hanging up her apron, and motioning for them to return upstairs. "But when my mother died . . . " Her voice falters. She takes a few steps upwards, keeping her face turned away from her friend.

When they reach the ground floor, she continues. " . . . when she died . . . on the day I was born . . . he started walking the streets to work off his grief." Her voice gains in strength. "He went everywhere. He told me he saw misery like he had never imagined; misery that more than matched his own."

They move to the dining room table again.

"I am his only child, and he wants me to grow up to care for others and make a difference in their lives, whether I'm a girl or not. He teaches me as often as my governess does. Maybe she shouldn't even be called that. She was very carefully chosen and doesn't live with us, just teaches me girlish things I need to know. Father has me read all sorts of things other girls aren't allowed. You can ask me any political question! I can cook and sew and run without growing pale. He says I should be able to vote, and I'm allowed to stay home alone and do nearly anything I want."

Her voice grows softer.

"It's quiet here. We don't have many people call. Father says I need to be shielded from . . . my outings are to work-houses and soup kitchens, and my books are my friends."

Sherlock detects her sadness. The lark flutters its wings and she looks up at the cage.

"We purchased Blondin, there, from a bird dealer south of the river. Poor thing has a broken wing. I want to let him go, but father says he would perish in London."

Her sadness doesn't linger. The boy's desperate situation seems to connect to everything she and her father believe in, and soon she is pressing him to tell her more about the murder case.

There is a sound at the front door. They sit very still, Sherlock poised to flee. *Silence.* Perhaps it was just a pebble or a piece of metal from a harness, thrown from the street by the wheel of a passing carriage. Irene turns back to the boy, now even more anxious to hear more about his troubles before her father returns.

He had planned to keep the most important details from her, but when she asks so earnestly, he can't hold back. He needs to tell someone, and his trust in her is growing.

"There are things about this crime that I wasn't able to speak about in jail," he begins.

He tells her Mohammad's whole story, outlines the information he has that might help him: about the crows, the eyeball, the police theory, everything. But everything doesn't seem like much when he describes it. What does he really have? Just a few crows muttering at the crime scene . . . and a glass eye. What is that compared to the evidence compiled against the accused? The police have the murder weapon, found concealed under Mohammad's coat. They have his bloody footsteps going from the scene to the shop. And on top of everything, Sherlock doesn't have *absolute* proof that the Arab is innocent – he thinks of Adalji's angry expression in the jail last night.

It seems to him that Irene believes everything he says, which makes things worse for her. If she had thought both he and the Arab guilty, she could have offered forgiveness and convinced him to turn himself in. But because she suspects he is innocent and caught in a deadly trap from which he might not break free, she is almost compelled to help him.

Only one thing about her truly disappoints him. He wants to know what the papers have been saying about the crime, but it turns out that the Doyles read only the stodgy *Times* of London. No sensation for them: no *News of the World*, no *Penny Illustrated Paper*, and certainly no *Police News*. Sherlock's "scandal sheets" hadn't known the identity of the murder victim during those first few days, and after a brief and restrained interest *The Times* said little about the crime: such lurid fascination was beneath them. Irene can't recall the dead woman's name or even her occupation.

He is back in the dog kennel well before Andrew Doyle returns home. John Stuart Mill will be kept in the house today, and Irene will try to control his whereabouts over the next while. The maid usually feeds the dog inside anyway. A cloth hangs down over the kennel's entrance, nearly touching the ground, obscuring the view from the back windows.

Sherlock lies awake until he sees all the lights go out in the Doyle house. He waits for what he guesses is an hour and then rises. Even if he actually wanted Irene to come with him, he wouldn't take a chance on entering the house to signal her. He leaves the yard and moves down the passageway.

She is standing across the road, leaning against the gold-tipped wrought-iron fence that surrounds the Museum grounds.

"I'm coming," she says clearly.

Almost as shocking as her presence in the night is her clothing. She appears to be wearing trousers.

"They're father's," she says curtly, not even looking down at them. "They shrank in the latest wash and he thinks I threw them out."

They are tied tightly around her waist with what appears to be a belt from a bathrobe. All her clothes are dark. Smart girl. But from the neck up she still glows like an angel: that blonde hair looks like a light, shining around her in the night.

"Shall we go?"

Perhaps this isn't a bad turn of events, thinks Sherlock. *The police will be looking for a tall, thin boy . . . on his own.*

They search for a long time without finding any scent of the Irregulars. Irene moves like a pale apparition beside him as they descend into the London night, mortified by the ghoulish scenes around her. Still, she keeps up to him and never mentions her fear. Sherlock watches every shadow. Tonight he is both hunter and hunted.

Down a dark Westminster street, they hear a shout directed their way.

"You lot!"

It comes from behind. Irene turns and sees a policeman running toward them. They freeze. The Bobbie rushes past, sounding his rattle, in pursuit of two loud, drunken soldiers, who stagger away in the distance and disappear around a corner. Sherlock finally lets out his breath.

Not long afterward, they catch sight of an Irregular – a lone miscreant on Wild Street near Drury Lane. It is one of the younger ones and he is scurrying east. The gang is likely on the alert and moving tonight after their little encounter

with the police fewer than twenty-four hours before. Sherlock
pulls Irene against the buildings every time the Irregular,
sensing someone trailing, turns to look back. They stay hot
on his meandering route all the way to Lincoln's Inn Fields.
This is the largest square in London. Prime Ministers have
lived in the big homes that line its exterior. But at night-
time, inside its iron fence and among the shadows created
by its many giant trees, thieves find perfect harbor. Sherlock
spies the Irregulars ensconced on the grass at the north-east
end. Malefactor is standing in front of them, addressing the
corps, holding an iron lock high in the air.

"Picking locks." he intones. "First one needs two
sharp objects." He produces a couple of ladies' hatpins,
one expertly bent at its tip. "Insert both into the lock."
Malefactor does so with a single hand, like a magician.
"Feel inside with your specialized tool. Each tumbler needs
to be pushed up and away from the cylinder to clear it,
each tumbler must fall into place. It is simple geometry."
Malefactor feels around with the bent hatpin. A smile
crosses his lips. He turns the other tool . . . and the lock
springs open.

"Presto!" he says. But almost instantly, he frowns. He
can feel the presence of intruders.

"You were followed!" he barks at his young charge.
Then he gathers himself and turns to the emerging figures.
"Master Holmes, I perceive."

But he doesn't tear into the half-Jew.

Sherlock has never seen such a look on his face.
His dark features seem to lighten, reflected in the glow of

Irene Doyle. For an instant he loses his composure. It is hard to believe he is capable of such a thing. He swallows so hard Sherlock can see his Adam's apple bouncing.

"Miss," he says, sweeping his battered hat from his head. "Miss," he repeats. "Whom do we have the pleasure of . . . "

"This is Irene . . . "

"Shut up, Holmes!"

"Miss Irene Doyle," she says, feeling uneasy both about him and the scene around her, yet trying to smile.

"Welcome, Miss Doyle. I am known as Malefactor and these are my associates." He motions to them and speaks through clenched teeth. "Stand up in the presence of a lady, you scum!"

They all leap to their feet.

"Why have you brought her here, Holmes?" he asks, returning to his pleasant voice. He is incapable of taking his eyes from her.

"She helped me escape."

Malefactor beams.

"She doesn't normally do things like that. Her father is a respectable man who believes in helping the unfortunate, not in judging, but helping."

"He sounds like a fine gentleman, Miss."

Irene seizes the moment. "Master Holmes needs your help."

The young criminal takes his eyes from her only for an instant to glance at Sherlock, then looks back.

"I was once more than I am now, Miss, and I will be more again some day. I am at your service."

Sherlock doesn't need any more invitation than that. They slip into the darkest part of the Fields and crouch low. First, Holmes gives Malefactor his information: dimensions inside the Bow Street jail, the habits of the turnkeys, and how he got out. Then he turns to the murder. He explains everything he knows, including how he found the glass eye. Malefactor simply nods his head and closes his eyes. After a while, he opens them and begins to focus.

"Several things. There are some details I *may* possess about this crime. I shall give you none. As to what you might do about it yourself: first, you need to be incognito. You need a disguise. I suggest cutting your hair very short, getting out of those clothes – we'll find you some – and putting some grime on your face." He knows the obsessively clean Sherlock will hate that. "You will work at night from now on. And you need that eye. You must go and get it, whatever the danger. Lastly, you must find the purse. When you find *it*, you will have the solution."

Malefactor's helpful attitude is surprising. Sherlock suspected that the master thief might find the situation intriguing, might think it good fun to meddle in all of this and see how things turn out (perhaps in the half-Jew's death), and offer some sort of small return in exchange for the Bow Street jail information. Sherlock also wondered if Malefactor might finally consider him one of his own and help out a fellow "criminal." The young Napoleon of crime believes in the code of the street: the shadows look out for each other. But his interest is beyond anything Holmes had hoped for. He wonders why. His answer comes immediately.

"Bring Miss Doyle when you return with a report," Malefactor smiles, turning to her. His face grows sterner as he glares back at Sherlock. "Just give me a report, is that clear? Expect no further assistance. I cannot help you more than I shall tonight. The Irregulars and I . . . this isn't our game." He turns aside. "Suitcase please."

The blond, silent Crew, who knows their inventory well, goes to a nearby cart. It overflows with stuffed boxes, trunks, cases and other valuables – a cache of stolen goods. He examines the selections and then plucks one out, like a professor choosing the perfect book. Malefactor nods to him and seizes a wooden chair.

"Come, Master Holmes. We are ready for your disguise. You may keep your trousers. The Peelers only look from the waist up and mostly at the face."

Sherlock is placed in the chair. Crew, dressed in his oversized, once-scarlet military tunic, opens the suitcase and picks out a dark shirt, a bulky black coat, and a blue kerchief. He searches around again and produces a navy blue cap like a sailor might wear. Malefactor nods again and Crew pulls off Sherlock's coat, undoes his cloth necktie, and motions for him to remove his linen shirt. Irene turns away. The old clothes are tossed on the cart and the new ones thrown onto his lap. Sherlock puts them on, then ties the kerchief around his neck. He can barely stand it. The clothes are filthy.

"Sit down," says the leader with a smile, enjoying the boy's discomfort. He pushes Holmes onto the chair again. "You need some grooming."

Grimsby steps forward, producing a pair of rusty scissors out of a deep pocket in his overcoat. With a grin, he takes his customer roughly by the head and begins to snip violently. Great hanks of black hair drop to the ground and in minutes there is a transformation. Sherlock's usually perfect hair is now only a few inches long in most places and less than an inch in others – uneven, as though someone has cut it by tearing it. But the disguising effect is magnificent. Sherlock can sense it. He knows he must be whomever and whatever he needs to be.

"And last but not least," says Malefactor.

Another gang member has a sack in his hand. This rake-thin little lad with ears like the handles on a teacup, a streaked face and bare feet, is the dirtiest of the Irregulars. He reaches into the sack, pulls out a piece of coal, throws the rest on Sherlock's lap and then tips the boy's head up. The urchin proceeds to draw deep, black lines around Sherlock's eyes.

When the sooty Irregular steps back, Irene draws in her breath. A street waif sits in front of her.

Malefactor is pleased with his dusty creation. "Disguise is an invaluable tool in the game of crime. It shall stand you in good stead. My information is that your mother is a singing instructor. You must have some acting in your blood. Use it. Fit your movements, your whole person, to your costume."

He turns and gazes at Irene as if he hopes she is impressed, then reluctantly steps back. The Irregulars begin fading into the night. The meeting has come to an end.

The boss vanishes too, though his disembodied voice registers in the night.

"*You are looking for an unexpected villain.*"

Sherlock doesn't say much as he walks back to Montague Street with Irene and barely remembers to look out for anyone pursuing. Her fear is outweighed by her astonishment at what she has seen. It is as if she entered another world with Sherlock Holmes and is returning with someone else. She wants to talk about his disguise and Malefactor and his advice, about all of it. But the boy's mind is far away.

An unexpected villain?

That could be anyone: a man, woman, or child – even Adalji. But the gang leader is absolutely right about the eyeball. Sherlock must get it back.

There is only one way to do it. The police are looking for him; they know all about his parents and where they live. If they catch him, they may hang him. But somehow . . . he has to go home. He can't speak with his mother and father. He must get in and out like a thief.

HOME ROBBERY

When he rises the next night he is ready to rob his own home. Irene has kept him fed all day, and steered the maid and the governess away from the back windows. In a few minutes, he expects to see her again. But when he comes out to the street, she is nowhere to be seen. She knows he has to do this alone.

He pulls his cap down over his forehead and heads south. His charcoaled eyes look out from under the brim. On the way, he practices walking differently. He is a street person now. Malefactor was right about his mother. Fascinated by the operatic stage, she loves to talk about the art of playing roles.

"You have to become a character when you are presenting a part. The audience has to believe that you are someone else."

The police have to believe he is from the streets. He walks slower, with a shorter step, imagining someone who has nowhere to go.

It has been more than a week since he's been to Trafalgar. He desperately wants to see it again: a leisurely stroll along Oxford Street and down to the Square. But those days are over. If the Bobbies know anything about his habits, they'll know the places he frequents. The Force often uses detectives disguised in everyday clothes. He makes for the river in a direct line and crosses at Waterloo instead of Blackfriars. Before long he is over the bridge and back in Southwark.

He sticks to the smaller streets, alert in the rookeries, ready to fight for his life in the dark Mint neighborhood. But it is an unusually cold, late spring night, the misty rain is uncomfortable in the fog, and fewer denizens are about. By the time he reaches the street next to his, his heart is pounding. He stays in the shadows, up against the buildings, in doorways. No one seems to be following.

But now, two people are coming toward him in the distance. Indistinguishable at first in the drizzle, he soon sees that they are boys, wearing just shirts and trousers, their dirty caps soaked right through. He spies them before they spot him and drops behind a broken-down wooden barrow that's been left to rot to the side of the footpath. He wonders why these two are out of doors at this hour; they are looking around as if searching for something, peering into alleys.

"I'm tellin' you, the Peelers is offerin' a fiver for him," says one, a lad named Crippen whom Sherlock despises. Crippen is a dustman's son who likes to tease Holmes about his breed. The other is a doughy waterman's boy, a follower. "Lor', a fiver!" he cries, "I'd turn over me mam and bulldog for that, let alone Sherlock Holmes."

They near. Sherlock feels a piece of cobblestone by his foot. He picks it up and heaves it to the other side of the road. They cross to investigate. He rises and slips around the corner, onto his street and out of their sight.

The dilapidated old hatter's shop comes into view. He looks up and sees the floor above it – his parents' little bedroom is there at the front. *His mother . . . his father.* A tear falls to his cheek. He wipes it in disgust and darts across to the alley at the back of the buildings. As far as he can tell, there's no sign of anyone watching, police or civilians. Perhaps the Force doesn't expect him to be this reckless.

He goes over the crumbling wall like a snake. The first foot he places on the rickety stairs is set down gently. He places another and starts to climb, at a measured but steady pace. He stays as low as he can. Will his parents' door be locked? Has his arrest put so much anxiety into their lives that they now fear the outside world much more than before? He reaches for the latch. It opens.

Perhaps he can take a chance: wake them and talk with them, assure them that he's well. They will know he's escaped. The police will have been here and . . .

A thought rushes into his mind. What if a detective is *inside* waiting for him? What if they've stationed a Bobbie there? Once he'd made the landing, he'd considered himself home free.

He opens the door carefully and lowers himself to the floor.

All is silent.

He can smell the cold fire, his mother's cooking, their clothing, and Wilber's pipe.

If there is a Peeler in the flat, maybe Sherlock can smell him too. He sniffs like a bloodhound. He listens. He can hear people sleeping. It sounds like two, just two – Wilber's snore in the bedroom and Rose's gentle breathing – but he can't be sure. In the dark flat he might as well be blind.

Sherlock wants to go to the little bedroom first, find his parents, likely sleeping in their clothes on this cold night, snuggle in between them on their little bed, forget all the evil in the world, speak with them in whispers, show them that . . .

"*You need that eyeball.*" Malefactor had said. "*You must go and get it whatever the danger.*" The gang leader is right. This trip is about getting in and out of the house as quickly as possible, unseen by the police and even his parents. The less his mother and father know, the less danger for everyone.

He crawls across the floor on his belly, stopping every few yards. His bed is at the far side of this main room that functions as their kitchen, parlor, dining room . . . and his bedroom. It won't take long. He prays that his mother hasn't found the eye. Maybe she's thrown it out with the slop pot. Or even worse, maybe the police have discovered it.

He feels a leg: the front leg of his bed near the wall. He is at the right end. The eyeball was left near where his head usually lies, which should be immediately above him. His fingers walk up the leg and feel for the worn pillow. They walk under the flat straw mattress.

There it is!

The eye is in his hand. He jerks it out quickly.

But someone stirs.

On his pillow.

He freezes and instantly knows who it is. He doesn't need a bloodhound's nose . . . it is her perfume . . . the faint scent of beer. Rose Holmes is lying in his bed.

He holds the eyeball close and slides under the frame. He hears her rise. Her bare feet come down in front of his face.

"Sherlock?" she asks. She sits for a long time listening to the stillness. Then she sighs.

"Stupid cow."

This time he can't stop the tear. It rolls out an eye, along his upper cheekbone and splashes to the floor.

"Stupid cow . . . he's gone."

She falls back into bed.

He lies there for what seems like an hour, hearing her sobbing, and then tossing and turning. Finally, she seems to settle and drift off. He counts to five hundred before sliding out. It is time to make for the door. But he can't resist. He gets to his knees and looks at his mother. She is indeed asleep, thank God. Her eyes aren't moving under her lids.

She has no dreams anymore.

He kneels in front of her for a long time, just looking at her. She is *so* near him. He could just reach out and kiss her on the cheek.

No. He can't.

He swivels and moves across the floor on all fours like a rat. Then he notices something. In the darkness, he can just make out his father's record book on their little table.

Wilber uses it to keep track of his legions of Crystal Palace birds. His square pencil is lying beside it.

Sherlock takes the pencil in his hand . . . and carefully draws a crow on the table.

Seconds later he is out the door and down the steps. It takes no time at all to leave his neighborhood, rush through the winding streets, run over Waterloo Bridge, and move up through the city to Montague Street, back to his dog kennel.

The only thing that makes him pause on the way is a copy of the *Daily News*, which he retrieves from a dustbin. But the crime appears to have left the London papers. They have their victim, their murderer, and prosecution is certain. They are saving their ink for the hanging. And it will come soon.

There's an unwelcome greeting at Montague Street, in the form of John Stuart Mill. He's lying on his back in his little house with his legs in the air, snoring, smelling worse than the Thames. The Corgi has decided to sleep out tonight and Irene obviously hasn't been able to convince him to do otherwise. Sherlock sighs and then snuggles in beside the fat little beast, finding that the only way to sleep is to take this foul canine into his arms. They barely fit inside their cramped quarters and Sherlock's long legs are twisted like the seaweed he's seen wrapped around Ratfinch's eels. One of his legs actually sticks out the door. J.S. Mill isn't a polite bedfellow either. Rude noises come from him in the night. Sherlock is appalled.

Isn't it enough that he has to wear such filthy, inelegant garments? Now he has to sleep with this gas bag.

When Irene wakes him in the morning, he is still snuggling the dog, the eyeball in one pocket, his hand clamped firmly over it from the outside. J.S. Mill is fast asleep.

She takes Sherlock indoors. He desperately wants to wash, but knows he shouldn't. He has to stay in disguise.

It is a lesson day for her, but still early. She has time to talk before her governess arrives. Her father has been gone for more than an hour.

Irene feels a thrill growing inside her. Sherlock actually has the glass eye. She can see it bulging in his pocket. And she can tell that a plan is growing in his mind: the look in his eyes is calculating.

They sit at the dining room table again, the chandelier above, the silver candelabra on the laced cloth atop the varnished table's surface, little Blondin in his cage nearby. They must make some progress, and keep their eyes on the front door.

"My father says that you need to have logic as your first principle in everything you do," begins the boy, sitting gingerly, aware that his clothes might soil the beautiful French chair. "My weapon against my apparent fate, and Mohammad's, is my brain."

Irene almost giggles, aware of his discomfort at being unclean and amused by his very grown-up way of speaking.

His observational skills don't include noticing subtle reactions in the opposite sex, so he continues without pausing.

"First things first," he intones. "We simply need more evidence. And we must find it by thinking before acting. Searching for it is one thing, but we have to search intelligently. Then, if we can gain more clues or know more about the clues we already have, we can begin to put together a theory. In the end, we have to prove that theory beyond *any* doubt."

Irene leans forward, "We need to eliminate the things that couldn't possibly have happened and work on the things that are most likely."

Sherlock smiles. He has never met a girl quite like this. The ones he knows are much rougher, much more apt to laugh at him. Irene has gone to the heart of the problem instantly. Her appetite for the sort of thing that interests him is obvious. He arrests his smile before it grows too evident. She lowers her eyes and adjusts the ribbon at the back of her head.

He thinks he'll startle her with something . . . impress her. "So," he proclaims airily, "Mohammad can't possibly have done it. That's our starting point."

His statement has the desired effect.

"But, why couldn't he have done it?"

"Because I'm guilty if he did . . . and because of the crows."

"I don't understand."

"He has to be innocent in order for me to be innocent. If he killed that woman and the purse isn't recovered, then the police are going to include me in the crime. That's how they are looking at things, with blinkers on:

it was a street crime committed for money. I fit a whole profile, but more importantly, they saw him talking to me at the Old Bailey – only me, in a crowd of hundreds. In their minds, we are connected. Street people . . . " his voice grows angry, "low-lifes like Mohammad Adalji and Sherlock Holmes, killed her."

She starts to reach her hand across the table to him, but stops herself and adjusts the candelabra.

"But if Mohammad didn't do it," he continues, "I am very unlikely to be included. We have to prove that someone other than the Arab did this. Then we have to find that person."

"And the crows? What do they have to do with Mohammad's innocence?"

"You will have to be patient with me about that, Irene. I'll explain when I have more evidence."

She knows not to press him and goes on.

"Isn't the coin purse really the key anyway? Don't we need to find it, above everything else?"

"Correct." Sherlock smiles again. "But I have a feeling we won't find it, at least not until the solution is at hand."

"So, what is our plan?" asks Irene.

"Three things to begin: first, we have to go back to the murder scene and examine the area thoroughly."

Irene raises her eyebrows.

"Secondly, we have to make enquiries in that neighborhood. I doubt the police have done any questioning of consequence. They think they have their man. And thirdly . . . " He pauses. "Do you have a magnifying glass?"

It is a favorite tool of his. His father has one and taught him the subtleties of its use. In fact, his neighborhood fame as a sort of young Bow Street Runner investigator was sealed the day he found the butcher's mute bull terrier by using such a glass. The canine had somehow locked itself inside a seldom-used back room in the old hatter's shop, the size of a penny-post stamp. The next day Sherlock noticed a strange white hair on a hat, ran upstairs for the magnifying glass, and followed a trail of nearly invisible dog hairs to the room. The Holmes family had an incomparable Sunday dinner that week: meat on their table.

Andrew Doyle's study is above them on the first floor off the drawing room. Irene is back with the lens in a minute. While she is gone, Sherlock pulls the eyeball from his pocket and sets it on the table. Irene gasps as she sits down. There in front of her is the clue she has heard so much about. It makes her shudder. She can see the specks of blood on the glittering white surface. She hands the magnifying glass to Sherlock.

"Thirdly, we have to examine this." He begins turning the eyeball around, looking at every blood splat – his first chance to observe it closely. "If this eye could see . . . it would save my life."

"It's a strange color," says Irene.

"It is?" he responds and sets it down on the table. In his haste to look for details, he hasn't noticed the most obvious thing about it. The iris is brown, but a large fleck of startling violet knifes into it at the top, about a fifth of the entire ring.

"You're right." He scrutinizes it.

"The owner's other eye is like that," says Irene softly.

"Three key facts about our clue then," states Sherlock. "It was found near the crime, blood splattered, and has a brown iris with a violet fleck."

He trains the lens on the eyeball again, turning it, looking for anything out of the ordinary. He sees something.

At the back, opposite from the iris, he notices a little scratch. At least he thinks it's a scratch. He goes on examining the rest of the surface, but then comes back to it. . . . It's two scratches.

"Letters," he says out loud.

"What?" She can't see what he is looking at and moves closer to him.

He brings the eye up to the magnifying glass and moves it back and forth, trying to focus the scratches.

"There are two letters on the back of the eyeball."

Irene waits.

"L . . . E."

He sets the lens down. "What do you make of it?"

"The owner's initials?"

"I doubt it."

"The manufacturer's?"

"Who makes false eyes in London?" He knows the answer.

"Glass blowers? Medical suppliers?"

"Or someone who does both," he replies. "We need a city directory. They have them in the Guildhall Library and they list all the businesses in London."

But Irene isn't sure what this will ultimately accomplish.

"Even if we discover who made the eyeball," she reasons, "we still haven't solved anything, have we?"

Sherlock looks as if he were focusing on something far away and taps his fingers together.

"My father always says that if you think about the solution first when dealing with a scientific problem, you are doing things backwards. We need facts, Irene. Once we have a collection of clues, a trail that we can follow, then we can seek our solution. The letters on this eyeball are like pieces in our puzzle."

Miss Stamford will be at the front door in minutes, so they agree to meet late in the afternoon. Irene imagines they will rendezvous at the house so she draws in her breath when he tells her where to find him . . . in broad daylight, about tea time.

"Go to the East End, the poor area in Whitechapel. Take someone with you: someone who won't ask questions. Not your governess this time. Make yourself visible. I'll see you. . . . Just walk near the crime scene."

12

ALL THAT GLITTERS

S herlock rises from the dog's house in the early afternoon and heads for the East End. He has Andrew Doyle's magnifying glass in his pocket. He's charcoaled his eyes and made them dark, pulled the cap down over his brow, and affected the slow shamble of a homeless boy. He blinks in the sun like an animal not used to the light.

Murderers always return to the scene of the crime.

He read that once in *The Illustrated Police News*. He doesn't know if it is true, but he hopes the Metropolitan Police and their detectives at Scotland Yard don't believe it. They will be frustrated by now, perhaps intensifying their search. They know he won't leave the city, that he doesn't have the means. He needs to be as alert as a hunted fox.

His nervousness grows as he goes farther east. He tugs the cap down even tighter. He didn't expect to be this frightened. All around him is another noisy London day – the crowded foot pavements, the great mixture of people, the shouts, and the smells. He yearns for the time, just a week or so ago, when he was nobody.

He sticks to busy places, staying in the swarms all the way to the East End. Soon he is walking on Whitechapel Road.

"You!" cries a firm voice. "Been lookin' for you every-where in London!"

Sherlock nearly jumps out of his skin. A man is approaching him. The boy doesn't lift his gaze. *Keep moving*, is all he can think. *Get into the crowd and vanish.* He attempts to edge past, but the man blocks his way. "Not partial to a partickler pie?" asks the street monger, ushering the boy toward his barrow of fish and fruit pastries.

Sherlock sighs and moves on, leaving the pieman to pursue another customer. In a few steps the boy is moving quickly along Whitechapel again, like the suspect he is, his head down, but his eyes rotating like an owl's, noting every Bobbie, every person who looks back.

The crime scene is near. He turns from the main road onto narrow Old Yard Street. Then he sees the alley. *The* alley. It appears to his left, running west off the street just ahead. Fear courses through him again the instant it comes into view. It is hard to even think of what happened down this lane on that dark night.

Sherlock steels himself. The crowds were thick on Whitechapel Road and at this time of the day a mixture of people move along Old Yard Street too. *Blend in as best you can*, he tells himself. Not like the police, whom you can spot at a distance. He often wonders why they are so regular in their habits and so obvious in their appearance.

Even the detectives in disguise can be picked out without much trouble.

He glances in both directions and then slips down the passage. It looks different during the early afternoon: deserted and not so spooky. He can see its dead end against the brick wall of another building. There are the old stable doors to his right. In this light, they look like they've been closed up for centuries.

The stain on the cobblestones is still visible. It is halfway down the passage, the rubble a bit farther. What sort of place is this for a murder? Is it a place where someone was taken . . . dragged . . . or is it a spot where two people agreed to meet? Did the murderer know the woman? Sherlock looks at the sheer expanse of the stain. There was anger in the deed. There was passion. This wasn't done for money, not for a mere coin purse. But if that is true, why is the purse gone?

He shakes off those thoughts. Observe, he tells himself. Deal with the evidence first. Find it.

A noise rings out and he starts. Turning back to the narrow street, he sees an old tinker walking toward Whitechapel, pushing his cart. Sherlock watches him limp past. In seconds there is movement out there again: a well-dressed gent, a lady on his arm. She glances at Sherlock, stares for a second with a hint of fear in her face, but then is guided forward and disappears. He imagines her perfume hanging in the air. Why would her gentleman bring her here? A shortcut, he guesses, toward a better street, or perhaps a charitable visit to a nearby workhouse?

He imagines the murdered young woman – beautiful, looking like his mother in her youth – entering this alley on that terrible night. It would be nearly pitch black. He smells the perfume she wears as it wafts in the cold London darkness. Why did *she* come here? What sort of woman would be compelled to this place in the night? Who saw her . . . who smelled *her* perfume?

There is a flutter on top of the building that forms one of the alley's walls.

Crows.

There are two of them. They observe him, their heads bobbing up and down as if saying hello to an old friend. One swoops to the ground, bold as brass. First it lands near the rubble where Sherlock found the eyeball. Very quickly, it seems uninterested. Then it waddles down the passage, walking on a line toward the street. It seems to have little fear of the boy, though as it nears, it flaps a few feet high and passes by, moving almost all the way to the street. Then it turns back toward him and resumes its stroll, as if keeping one eye on him and the other on the ground, occasionally pecking and scratching.

The crow is looking for something. *Again.*

Sherlock advances toward it. It suddenly rises into the air, as if it can see out the back of its head, and flies up and settles on top of the building again next to its mate. They peer down.

The boy glances around. People continue passing on the street, but no one turns or stops at the alley – no one seems to be looking his way. He carefully follows the crow's path, leaning over with his face close to the ground. No obvious clues have been left on the dirty cobblestones. There are signs of footprints, but they are faint, just indistinct collections of the marks of footwear left by all sorts of people: the victim, her murderer, policemen, even his own broken-down boots. A cart's tracks obscure them further.

Behind him, the crow drops down into the alleyway again. It begins crisscrossing the passage. Sherlock turns and watches it.

Two facts occur to him: first, it's after something it finds attractive, something it can't leave alone; second, it doesn't know exactly where that thing is.

What would it find irresistible? Not the purse, surely. It doesn't know about money. A purse wouldn't be any more attractive to it than a glove or a hat.

Something *shiny* again: something just as interesting as that eyeball.

Jewelry. Good jewelry – a piece that glows so seductively a crow can't let it be.

He thinks for a moment about how the bird is searching the area. It has taken two approaches. First, it followed a path, like the one the woman and her murderer took down the passageway. Now, it is searching randomly.

Why randomly?

Instantly a piece of the puzzle falls into place.

In the violent struggle, an item of jewelry must have come loose and been thrown somewhere in the alley. Who did it belong to . . . the woman or the person who killed her? *Find it first*, he reminds himself.

He advances on the crow. It flies up again and lands overhead. This time it and its mate mutter at him. Sherlock decides to try something reckless.

He looks toward the street: the odd person passing. . . . No one looking.

He regards the bloodstain once more and imagines where the woman might be standing: likely with her back to the dead end as she waits to meet someone. In a struggle, where would jewelry fly? He narrows it down to an area about eight feet by eight, closer to the dead end than the rubble of bricks. He takes out the magnifying glass, glances back at the street, then drops to all fours, the glass held close to his eyes.

Sherlock looks for a long time. Too long. His knees are getting sore, so he gets to his feet.

The crow screams.

The boy glances behind him.

His foot had knocked something ajar when he stood up. It is a heavy old horseshoe leaning against the wall and there beside it, partially underneath, something the size of a sovereign is glinting. He scrambles to pick it up. When he puts his hand on it, he realizes that there is more to it than he first thought. Some of it is jammed behind the horseshoe, stuck between it and the wall. He tugs and it slithers out, like a glittering snake. A bracelet. It looks delicate, like it would fit a pretty wrist, and it seems expensive, a luxury item. Diamonds and little silver charms hang from it. Sherlock examines them. One of them is an eye.

The crows are upset. They caw and squawk and look like they want to descend on Sherlock. Up the alleyway on Old Yard Street, two tradesmen stop, look toward the black birds and then down at the boy with the dirty face. He instantly pockets the bracelet.

It is time to move.

He wants to run, but doesn't. He takes on his street character and shamble. Wishing he could glance everywhere, he holds his gaze down and moves. Who are these onlookers? At the entrance to Old Yard Street he takes a hard right. The men don't follow.

But then he sees another man, this one large and thick, dressed in the black livery of a coachman, two thin vertical slashes of red on his coat, standing still across the street, staring in his direction, then looking up at the shrieking crows as if startled by them. Sherlock can't see his face because a shadow is cast across it. A *detective*? Would the police use that disguise?

He races toward Whitechapel, then turns onto it, desperate to disappear into its crowds. A hand grabs him from behind.

"Sherlock!"

It's a higher-pitched voice than he feared . . . that smell of soap, the slender arms.

Irene.

She's been waiting. She nods to someone who is walking with her, probably a servant who once worked for her father. The man pretends to not see the boy – a skill particular to experienced domestic help – and fades into the crowd.

"Did you find anything?" she asks.

Sherlock glances back toward Old Yard. His heart is racing. The big coachman in black livery seems to have vanished. Did Sherlock imagine him? Was he a ghost?

"I've . . . I've been here too long," he says through clenched teeth. "Act like I'm begging and you're giving me something. Reach into your purse. Hand me a penny!"

She does. He sweeps his cap from his head and bows.

"You didn't answer me. Did you find something?"

"Yes."

"Yes?"

"We can't talk here. We need to be where it might seem reasonable for you to be speaking with a street person . . . a big church."

"St. Paul's," she answers immediately.

"I'll meet you on the front steps where the crowds are."

She takes the direct route and pretends she is with others. He swings south, toward the Thames, and approaches the cathedral from the river. As he walks, he realizes that he has put himself in even more danger. Now he is a black-faced street boy . . . with a lady's diamond bracelet in his pocket.

❧

"What did you find?" she asks the instant he arrives.

They are at the top of the big stone steps near the pillars and high wooden doors at the magnificent entrance. There are many street people nearby, some in bare feet, pleading for food and money. Gentlemen wearing tall hats and ladies in long, silk crinoline dresses are pausing as they climb the stairs, handing coppers to children. Sherlock motions to Irene to move into the shadows under the columns. It feels cold here, even in the warmth of the day.

"This," says Sherlock, glancing around, then drawing the long glittering bracelet from his pocket.

Irene gasps, bringing her hand to her mouth. "It's beautiful."

"There's an eye on it."

Irene takes it into her hand for a moment. Her face seems to glow in its reflection.

"What do you think it tells us?" she asks.

"It might mean she was rich, or it might not. She might have simply owned this single, expensive thing. . . . Or maybe it belonged to the person who killed her. . . . "

Irene's face turns pale. "A woman?"

"It connects the two of them," says Sherlock.

Irene wonders exactly how. But she doesn't ask him to explain. She knows this isn't the right time. She also knows she shouldn't try to comprehend this remarkable boy, that that is the way to be his friend. One understands him by not understanding, by trusting his mind. When they're home, he'll tell her more.

Sherlock is actually feeling pleased. Not just because he is beginning to see things about this murder – see a possible path through the labyrinth he has to get through to find a solution – but because he knows he has a friend standing beside him, a true friend for the first time in his life.

Then another light comes on in his brain like the beam on a locomotive. It frightens him to his boots.

"*They saw it*," he mumbles.

His whole face has changed: a look of horror has come over it.

"What?" she asks, unsettled by his expression.

"They saw it," he says again.

"Who?"

"The crows."

"Saw what?" She knows the answer but wants him to go on.

"I've been guessing that the crows were there when it happened." He pauses, staring down the elegant white steps. "Now . . . I *know* they were. They saw the *whole* thing."

Sherlock's eyes turn to hers. His black pupils are huge.

"They watched this person . . . murder her."

13

SEEING EVIL

Sherlock won't explain until they get back to Montague Street. He seems petrified. He stares ahead as if he were watching the murder transpire from the top of one of the buildings, watching with the eye of a crow.

Irene walks about half a football pitch in front of him, occasionally glancing back to make sure he is following. Up they go from St. Paul's through bustling central London and back into her quiet neighborhood. Sherlock stops well down the street as she steps through the squeaky, wrought-iron gate and moves up the stone stairs to the front door. If it is unlocked, her father is home.

She tries the door. Locked. Feeling for the key in her purse, she looks down the street toward Sherlock and motions. A few minutes later they are sitting on the settee in the small morning room on the ground floor with John Stuart Mill stretched flat nearby. Irene is positioned in a big window to see both ways on the street. Sherlock is hidden from view by a scarlet curtain.

Andrew Doyle will be home any minute. But she has to know.

He starts talking as soon as they sit.

"The first thing I realized when I got there was how wide the bloodstain was . . . which likely means the murderer knew his victim, because it wasn't the quick kill-and-get-away job of a thief. It was a crime of passion – an angry one."

Irene adjusts her position and her long woolen dress on the cushioned settee. She has asked for this, wanted to get out from under the restrictions of her home and be with this boy pursuing justice. But now she is beginning to face the stark reality of it all.

Sherlock stops talking. His mind is drifting off again, trying to see the murder. Irene brings him back.

"But how do you know the crows saw it happen? Maybe when the sun came up the next morning and shone into the alley, they happened by and noticed part of the eyeball and even the bracelet glittering in the ground. Or maybe they *were* there that night, nearby anyway, but simply heard the woman scream, or saw some commotion and were drawn to the alley. Then they noticed the woman lying there, bits of glitter on the ground near her. They flew off in fear, but kept coming back to find their prizes and were always spooked whenever people appeared. It's impossible to know how much they saw. Impossible. You had to have been there."

"*I know what they saw,*" murmurs Sherlock. His long white fingers are entwined. He squeezes them tightly together.

"*How* do you know?" She asks intently.

"There was a crow on one of the buildings when I got there. I watched him. He did three things. He checked the rubble where I found the eyeball, he walked up and down the passage toward the street and back, and he moved around randomly on the side of the alley opposite from the stain."

Sherlock peeks around the curtain and looks outside, then leans closer to Irene.

"The crow didn't spend long where the eyeball had been because he could see it was gone. Then he started searching for something else . . . something that interested him, something that glittered. The fact that he looked near the spot where I found the bracelet was an indication that he saw the murder. . . . He knew that it was flung away during the struggle."

"But still," protests Irene, "couldn't he have just noticed the bracelet glittering in the cobblestones the way I suggested? Couldn't he have seen it lying there after the murder? Maybe he moved about randomly because he simply wasn't certain where it was?"

"I thought that too . . . for a while," says Sherlock. "And you're right. What I've said only tells us that the crow *may* have seen something flung across the alley . . . it isn't proof."

"So . . . what is?"

"The crow walked up and down the alley . . . " he leans so close to Irene that their noses almost touch, " . . . on a *direct line* from the bloodstain to the street."

Irene shudders. Sherlock is right. The crow *must* have seen the victim or the killer or both enter the alleyway from the street and walk a direct line toward the murder scene . . . or, at the very least, it saw the villain rush back to the street after completing his horrible deed. It *knows* where they walked.

The Whitechapel murder was *not* unobserved.

"*The crows saw it,*" she gasps.

The grandfather clock in the hall ticks.

"And *we* have to find a way to see it too," muses Sherlock.

He looks up and sees a frightened expression on her face. He can tell that she doesn't want to see this horrible act, not even in her mind. She wants everything to be over: for him to be free, Mohammad to be released, that poor woman to have peace, the real culprit to be brought to justice. Sherlock is different. He wants to see it all, every bloody moment. And he wants vengeance, for everyone.

But at that instant something nearly as frightening as the image in his mind appears on the street outside the window.

"He's here!" Irene cries.

Her father is approaching the front door. She's been so engrossed in their conversation that she's neglected her lookout duties.

"Out. Out!" she exclaims, rising to her feet.

Sherlock springs up and gallops out of the morning room, down the hallway, past the dining room, to the back door. He can hear Andrew Doyle opening the front entrance, taking off his hat, hanging up his umbrella.

"Irene?"

"Yes, father?"

She materializes in front of him like a spirit. Her voice is calm as she stands there in the doorway of the vestibule, blocking her father's view of the hall. His walrus mustache smiles.

Sherlock opens the back door, closes it gently, and makes for his dirty dog kennel. He wriggles into it and lies still, pulling his legs up so his boots don't show.

No sounds come from the house.

Sherlock finds it difficult to stay calm. His father has taught him that too much emotion is the enemy of the scientist. "Use cold, hard reason. Let it be your guide, my boy. Move slowly and accurately when you are seeking a solution." *That is fine*, he thinks, *when you are dissecting a frog or roasting some chemical on a Bunsen lamp, but this is life and death.* He has his mother's passion and can't help it. He wants to stand up, rip the dog kennel apart, scream at the world that he is no criminal, that Mohammad isn't guilty, that life isn't fair, that the real villain has to pay. Villains everywhere have to pay.

He wants to see the murder now!

He lets himself imagine. Black, oily feathers envelop him in the yellow fog of the wicked London night. He is perched on the edge of a building, but not on one in the alley. He is out on the street just off Whitechapel Road, on Old Yard. Down below, a woman comes hurrying along the street, the heels of her fancy laced boots smacking on the cobblestones as she looks around, desperate to get somewhere. She carries a small lantern that only dimly lights the darkness. She is young and beautiful and her white neck, ear lobes, and perfect soft hands *all* have diamonds.

Those crows, he is sure, saw the woman long before she was murdered. To them, she glittered in the night. Why else would they have been drawn to the scene? Because of a scream? That would frighten them.

She turns down the passage. She stops. Someone meets her, just as planned. Only then do the crows land on the building in the alley, still eyeing the glitter on the pretty, anxious woman. Then there are heated words. There is a horrible shriek and shining objects fly through the air. . . .

Sherlock can't see who did it . . . not yet.

What about the woman? He knows something about her now. She is wearing more than just a little jewelry. That may mean something soon.

It is time to move forward with their plan: have Irene check the city directories for every glass-eye manufacturer in London; find someone near the crime scene who heard something on that fatal night.

But his thoughts keep returning to the woman. Who was she? Why did she go there at that hour? Why would someone kill this particular person in cold blood on a dark East End street?

When Irene brings him food under her shawl at suppertime he asks if she can visit the Guildhall Library; and later, before odorous John Stuart Mill can be deposited next to him again, he slips out the backyard and goes to Lincoln's Inn Fields. He finds Malefactor nearby in a little lane, sitting on a rusted-out, overturned rain barrel against the back of a building, his Irregulars scattered along the wall. His moth-eaten top hat is perched at that jaunty angle on his sweaty hair, his tail-coat folded neatly beside him. In his hand is a notebook, one Sherlock has often seen him scribbling in. The outlaw enjoys inventing numerical problems to see if he can solve them. Sometime in his mysterious past, he had learned this: studied mathematics and been a whiz. "It keeps the mind sharp" he often says. "Prepares one's brain for the challenges of life." Though long aware that Sherlock is approaching, he simply glances up when the tall, thin boy nears and then looks down at his numbers again. It was made perfectly clear that he would provide the fugitive with no more help. All he expects tonight is information.

Sherlock may hang if he doesn't find the East End fiend, so he summons his courage and asks his question – carefully.

"I . . . need to know if anyone heard anything on the night of the murder. Could the Irregulars make enquiries in the East End?"

The brilliant young criminal gets to his feet and crosses his arms.

"Where's the girl?" He doesn't sound pleased.

"She couldn't be with us this evening."

The crime boss doesn't find that funny. He studies Sherlock's face.

"You should not be drawing her into this sort of trouble. I wouldn't."

"She wants to be involved."

"Why?"

"She believes in justice."

Malefactor laughs. "I doubt she's a fool."

"She's a caring human being."

The boy in the tall hat appears ready to deliver a punch. He stops himself by an obvious effort of will. He demands his report. Sherlock tells him what he's learned, picking and choosing details to reveal, hoping it is enough to please. When he is done, Malefactor regards him like a king deciding if his life should be spared, if any of this information is worthwhile putting into the Irregulars' vast mental log of underworld activities. Inquiries in the East End? It is *highly* irregular. But then the young crime lord thinks of the remarkable Irene Doyle and her plea for this wretched lad. If he turns down Holmes, she will know and think less of him. There is also an outside possibility that Holmes, if he doesn't get himself killed, can actually tell him something more about this murder – it's never a bad thing to be informed about such incidents. He looks away.

"I'll do this one thing . . . for the girl."

Sherlock stays out all night. He keeps pondering the murder victim. He has to know who she is and he has to know now. He needs to read his kind of papers.

He's been thinking about how many days have passed and by his calculations this is a Sunday morning. That gives him an idea. Before the sun rises he carefully makes his way toward the vendors he knows near Trafalgar Square.

Most of the newsboys, whether young or ancient, consider him a nuisance. In the past, he's attempted to steal papers when he couldn't find what he wanted in a bin. They'd spot him trying and pretend to call the police. One, who owned a bull terrier with a dark circle around its eye, once set that vicious brute upon him.

But there is one seller who is different, a poor legless chap with a misshapen face named Dupin, who sits on a low stool behind a rough, homemade wooden kiosk to hawk his papers, pitifully trying to look as respectable as he can. His deeply-lined face has been twisted from birth, his mouth constantly shows its yellow teeth – it is often hard to tell if he is happy or sad. Sherlock has seen him many times going home after work, transporting himself on a dirty little wooden platform with small iron wheels, his torso and the tools of his trade strapped to the surface. Dupin propels himself with hands protected by filthy, fingerless gloves, appearing like half a man – a ragged suit, a tie, a face, and a crushed bowler hat. He and the boy have spoken many times.

"Master Sherlock 'olmes?" he says in surprise in his raspy way, somehow knowing to keep his voice down as he notices the boy coming out of the shadows and drawing near. The cripple focuses to make sure he isn't being deceived. He is struggling to erect his big, torn umbrella over his crude little table and can't quite make it bloom. "You looks like a 'ellhound is after you, you do."

"That's about right," says Sherlock.

The tall, thin boy grips the umbrella by the stem and shoves it open.

"'eard you was in jail."

"You heard correctly." Sherlock is glancing around, keeping his head down.

The cripple looks up at the gangly lad. As usual, there is sympathy in his eyes. Sherlock marvels at this man: how he can care about others despite his lot in life.

"I'm wagerin' this ain't no social visit."

"I need a favor."

"For a million crowns, you've got it, guvna."

Dupin has a peculiar hobby. Most newsboys can't wait to dump their extra papers the minute their day is over, but he keeps a copy of every issue he's ever sold of both the glorious *Daily Telegraph* and his Sunday paper, the sensation-filled *News of the World*. In fact, he often keeps a few of each. He can recite from memory nearly every word in every paper going back several weeks at a time. Disraeli's speech on India? Tuesday, page 7, columns one through five, running over three columns onto 8. He is a veritable living index. Rumor has it he keeps a book that contains a brief biography of every person he's ever read about in the news.

A month's collection of papers is always near his side at his barrow and when he isn't shouting "*The Day-leeeeeeee! Tel-eeeeeeeeeeeeeeeee-graph!!*" at passersby, he rereads the recent news, committing it to memory.

Sherlock speaks quickly.

"I need what you have about the Whitechapel murder."

"Need it?" The cripple's expression narrows. "You mixed up in that someways?"

The boy shakes his head. "No. Others have mixed me into it."

"That will be a million crowns," says the little man quietly and moves to a stack of papers behind his cart: *The News of the World.* He runs his hand down their edges like a clerk consulting a file, expertly plucks out the perfect choice, last Sunday's thick paper, and hands it over as secretly as a dormouse.

"Thank –"

"Be off with you, Master 'olmes."

Sherlock walks quickly back to Montague Street, thinking about time and how little he has left. In less than two weeks Mohammad will be condemned. This paper *has* to tell him something.

John Stuart Mill's bulging carcass is stretched across the back of the dog kennel when the boy sneaks into it again. The snores are almost deafening. *This is going to be a challenge* thinks Sherlock, as he rolls the dog over several times like a baker worrying his dough. He gets him out of the way and nearer the door. The canine doesn't so much as stir. The boy props himself on the dog's round belly, positioning his newspaper in just the right way at the entrance to gain enough sunlight to read and still keep his head from view. Anyone peering down from the Doyles' windows will think they are simply seeing J.S. Mill in glorious repose.

The Illustrated Police News hadn't mentioned the victim's name for the first three days: something about her identity being unconfirmed and authorities trying to locate and notify possible next of kin. But now Sherlock is looking at the first *News of the World* that appeared directly following the murder, on the next Sunday, *six days* after it happened, sold on the streets when Sherlock was in jail. And it is a goldmine! The paper has leapt at the story. He runs his eyes hungrily down the first column until he finds something about the victim.

> "Rumors circulated, during days immediately following the crime, that she was an actress . . . "

That's strange, he thinks. He pauses to consider it. Why wouldn't an actress be quickly identified, especially one who, if Sherlock's theory is right, had the sort of income that allowed her to wear expensive jewels?

There is only one answer. This wasn't a rising star, no Ellen Terry or Nelly Farren. She had to be a bit player, someone nobody recognized at first glance, or about whom the general public doesn't particularly care. But that is only a partial answer. How could she have money? And who was she? He reads on.

> "Auburn hair . . . medium height . . . age twenty-two."

He wants more than that and turns the page, ignoring the gurgling sound from J.S. Mill's gut. There in front of him is a large woodcut drawing of . . . Lillie Irving.

"Lillie," he says out loud. At last. She is beautiful indeed. And almost the spitting image of his mother in her younger years. The boy swallows and keeps reading.

> "Miss Irving had appeared in numerous plays and pantomimes over the four or five years since she first entered the profession. Though a young woman of remarkable physical charms, she never ascended to any significant roles. She is dearly missed by fellow thespians, who say she came from humble parentage, that she lived alone in London, had no siblings, that her mother and father were recently deceased."

Sherlock has never heard of her. Whatever is on at The Lyceum, The Theatre Royal Drury Lane, anywhere in the West End or elsewhere, he likes to take note. That whole world of wonder fascinates him. But Lillie Irving? She doesn't even ring a distant bell.

How could an unknown like this, playing small roles given to her solely for her beauty, have been decked out in jewels that night, or on any night? She came from "humble parentage." Something doesn't make sense.

He reads farther down in the article.

"She was playing in *The Belle's Stratagem*, at the Theatre Royal Haymarket when she met her untimely death."

The Haymarket. He knows exactly where it is: not more than a costermonger's shout from Trafalgar; an area frequented by pleasure seekers of a questionable sort. Plays begin at 8:00 in London and finish past 10:00. He needs to know more about Lillie Irving.

He'll spend the rest of the day writing a script in his head – what he needs to do and say at the Haymarket. Then it will be time for a night at the theater.

He won't take Irene. He doesn't want her near a place where suspicions might touch her and directly involve her in this dangerous game.

He'll go alone.

14

LILLIE AND MR. LEAR

He doesn't need to change his disguise. The filthy clothes he has on will work perfectly. Crossing busy Leicester Square, he goes over his lines. He mumbles them aloud, less afraid of detection here, as he moves through the big crowd. This is one of the rowdiest spots in London. You can hide an elephant here. All around him are dandies and ladies, beggars and blokes, gypsies dancing, sounds coming out of the open doors of music halls, a steady buzz of talk in the air, drowning out the hiss of the gas lamps that dimly light the colorful scene.

After he turns down narrow Whitcomb Street he has to be more careful. The crowds thin. The theater is still in session. He tucks his head down and watches for anyone surveying pedestrians. He'll approach the building from the rear. He knows a spot.

He cuts through an opening between shops and in seconds sees the tall white back of the Theatre Royal Haymarket against the dark sky. Clouds are gathering in the night's ceiling, threatening rain again. He checks the fading moon – it must be nearing 10:00. The stage door is straight ahead. The shadows here will give him protection. He drops down between two dustbins. A big rat scurries away.

Laughter, then silence, then faint declamations of actors come through the stone walls. The reactions of the crowd make him smile. Sleep begins to descend on him. Applause. Sleep.

Suddenly the door opens. Feet are moving quickly.

Sherlock leaps up. His cap falls from his head and he nearly knocks over the bins. Straightening them, he tries to remember his lines. His mouth feels dry.

Luckily, the first person out the door isn't the sort he is seeking. It is a man. Sherlock recognizes his face. Not a big star – the famous ones leave through the front door in hansom cabs. Shrinking back, he lets the actor pass. Silence. The door opens again. Another man appears with a woman on his arm. They are wrapped up together, her lips are painted scarlet red, the top of her dress reveals part of her bare chest, his hand slides down her back and pinches her somewhere lower. She giggles. The door slams. There is silence for seconds. Then a woman appears alone. He's seen this lady's picture in the theater reviews – she wouldn't have associated with Miss Irving.

The door opens again. Out comes a beautiful young woman, nearly as pretty as Lillie, certainly as young. Sherlock has never seen her face before. He steps in front of her.

It is nearly a fatal mistake and he is only saved by the woman's pluck. She gasps, but doesn't scream. She pulls back her purse like a cricket bowler ready to fire, her target the boy's face.

"No," he protests, trying not to raise his voice. "I'm not a thief!"

"Then stand aside," she commands. She isn't delicate when frightened. Her face has colored.

Sherlock has stage fright. What is his first line?

"I . . . I am an acquaintance of Lillie Irving."

"You?" she lowers her purse.

That will do for an answer. She is on script.

"Miss Irving was a wonderful lady," Sherlock begins.

"She was," says the actress, her voice softening.

"I used to beg from her."

"I've never seen you before."

That is off script and she seems suspicious.

"Uh . . . not here . . . in Leicester Square. . . . She always gave me something."

"Well, she had extra, she did."

Sherlock doesn't speak. Best to see if the woman will say more.

"Her fancy man," she explains.

The boy remains mute.

"A mystery, he was." The woman seems to want to talk. "I was her best friend and knew naught. Usually we gossiped about our beaus. But that was how they wanted it, she and him. That's what she said, anyway. His footman sent his card up to her room in Aldgate one evening when I was there. Asked to be on my way, I was. . . . She was raised just east of there, poor thing." The woman smiles, "Yes, her *very* fancy man. . . . That's how she got them diam –"

The door opens again. An older actress enters the night, big and fat, makeup heavy on her face, her bosom nearly spilling out of her dress. She eyes the street urchin confronting her young friend.

"What's this?" she inquires loudly. "What's he want?"

"Just asking after Lillie, Maude. It seems he used to –"

"Lillie!" The big woman advances toward the boy, glaring at him. "Why would you be asking . . . "

Sherlock doesn't wait for more. He darts away, back down the opening between the buildings toward the streets. Behind him, he hears the fat woman chiding the younger one, telling her she is a "yapper . . . a young lamb with a big mouth." He sprints away like a derby horse, until he plunges into the crowds of Leicester Square.

Lillie had a fancy man! He gave her diamonds. What did Malefactor say when all of this began? What did he let slip about the murderer? "*He isn't on the loose.*" That's what he said. The word on the streets, the kind of information that Malefactor never shares with Sherlock, spoke of the *sort* who had committed this crime – it didn't bear the trademark of a professional killing, the villain wasn't of their ilk. This murderer is safe somewhere and has resumed a normal life. This person is wealthy!

Now he is getting somewhere.

He'd learned something else. "She was raised just east of there, poor thing . . . " the young actress had said. Now he knows why the villain had been able to draw her there. She lived in Aldgate and grew up to the east . . . in Whitechapel. Lillie Irving had known those streets.

His eyes blink awake. Birds are singing. It feels damp and warm. John Stuart Mill is nowhere to be seen – no bad smells. A third of a loaf of bread and a small mug of milk are inches from his nose. And there is a note. He snatches up the bread, sits with his back crouched against the dog kennel wall and bites off a piece. Even without the miserable mutt in here, his head nearly touches the ceiling and his legs feel cramped. But he pays little attention. He pulls back the cloth from the entrance, spreads out Irene's note on the ground and allows the morning light to hit it perfectly.

"This is what I discovered at the Guildhall Library," it begins in Irene's pretty hand.

Rushing past her next few words, he comes to what matters.

There are two columns: one a list of medical equipment suppliers in central London, another of glass blowers. He runs his finger down the first, about a dozen names. None start with either L or E, the two letters he'd found scratched on his glass eyeball. He searches the second: Boffin . . . Fledgeby . . . Headstone . . . Hexam . . . Lear . . .

Lear!

Lear Glass Blowing . . . Carnaby Street. It is in Soho and unexpected. It's far from the East End, just a short stroll from Mayfair and the wealthy residential districts.

But this is his only lead. He has to use it somehow.

Sherlock sits cross-legged in his cramped dog's house, plotting.

Mohammad Adalji is sitting too, over on Bow Street on his stone bed in the holding cell. He has been here for two weeks now, dreaming at night of sunny Egyptian skies. His only ray of hope is that tall, dark-haired half-Jewish boy, who told him a tantalizing tale of finding a false eye at the murder scene. But the boy vanished from this station four days ago and hasn't been found since. If the young Jew is out there, he is likely running, making himself scarce, his passing interest in justice long gone, Mohammad's only hope gone with him.

The Arab knows that the police keep him here instead of at the Whitechapel district station or Newgate Prison because they want him far from the East End. He imagines how the London public must loathe him. His trial is no more than a week or two away. He's been as much as told it won't go well. *Murderers are hanged right after trials.* He drops onto his knees on the hard stone floor. The jailers won't tell him exactly which way is east, so he has to imagine it. He turns in that direction and prays.

When Andrew Doyle is at home, Irene is careful about how she leaves food for her backyard lodger. She sets his meal on the steps. Sherlock always snatches it quickly, beating the lumbering J.S. Mill to it when he must. She appears about the same time every night.

Mr. Doyle is home this evening. When Irene slips away to the door and secretly sets the morsels outside, she feels a tug on her dress. Looking down, she spots Sherlock.

"Make me an eye patch," he whispers, "and meet me tomorrow morning."

Her governess is off the next day. Sherlock waits all morning for Irene to appear. Through the windows he can see her father moving about in the house, holding a thick book in his hand, questioning Irene about its contents. The boy is almost pleased to see that she may not be able to accompany him. Maybe his plan isn't wise. Maybe he needs another, safer idea. The morning turns to afternoon. Lying there curled up in the dog kennel, he falls into a daydream.

He thinks of his parents and drifts into that other time, before he was born. There she is, gorgeous and happy in a magnificent white silk dress, readying herself to see *The Thieving Magpie*. And there is his father, dressing for his first visit to the opera, and . . .

The Doyles' back door opens. Out comes Irene with a black eye patch in her hand. Sherlock edges toward the light and looks up.

"Father went to a meeting. He'll be gone for a while." She bends down to meet his gaze. "What are we doing?"

She seems excited, happy to be released from home again. That almost makes it worse.

"I'm not sure you should accompany me."

She gives him a look. It is stern, alarmingly like an expression his mother sometimes uses when she isn't pleased with something he's done. He realizes he has no choice.

"We will be shopping," he says, "for a glass eye."

He leaves first and they meet on the street. The black patch is over his left eye, just under his screwed-down cap.

Soho is a fabulous and daunting place. It is over-crowded, full of spidery streets, colorful characters, friendly ladies, food, and languages of every sort. A spirit of adventure is alive and multiplying. You can find nearly anything here.

They pass a loud English street band filling the air with brassy sounds, a conjurer playing tricks and shouting, and a fire-eater dressed in red satin who tilts his head back and dramatically lowers the flame to his lips from above, all the while watching Sherlock Holmes intently. *Why is he looking at me?* It unnerves the boy. He presses Irene to move faster. Soon their shop comes into view.

Lear Glass Blowing is a little establishment halfway down Carnaby Street with a latticed window extending across the storefront. A bell tinkles as they enter. A man with a bulbous head, big whiskers, a red face, and thin-ning salt-and-pepper hair steps from the back room to the counter. His teeth are gray and his hands nearly black. His eyes squint at the strange couple as though he were trying to bring them into focus – a well dressed young woman and a dirty street urchin with a patch over his left eye.

"May I be of service, Miss?" he enquires, smiling directly at the young lady. The street boy might as well not be there.

Sherlock is amazed at the acting abilities Irene displays. She is calm and collected and plays her role to perfection.

"I am here on a charitable errand. This young gentleman," she motions toward Sherlock, who keeps his head lowered just enough to be hard to recognize, "lost an eye as a child and has no means to replace it. I give him a few copper coins when I see him, but would like to do more."

"Yes?" asks the glass blower, still only regarding the young lady.

"Are you Mr. Lear, himself?"

"In the flesh," he smiles proudly, puffing out his chest, which barely extends beyond the big belly inside his dirty, blue-checked waistcoat. It is a big grin and those gray teeth are on display. He runs a blackened hand forward on his round, red head, smoothing down the thin hairs that flow over his pate. They look like the white worms that wriggle in the muck on the banks of the Thames.

"I am looking for someone who can make this boy a glass eye. Is that something you do?"

"It is, very much so. I would be glad to Miss . . . Miss?"

Irene says nothing. Sherlock has made her promise not to reveal her identity.

Lear continues. "I would be glad to, Miss, but the lad must see a doctor first."

His customers look disappointed.

"A doctor, Miss," he explains. "I make the false eyeballs, you see, for a medical supplier, Copperfield's just down the street here on Beak. But I never have anything to do with the patients. I can blow you a beautiful paperweight, my dear. How about one of them swans that Her Majesty has in St. James' Park?"

"That won't be necessary. I shall have him see a physician. Thank you."

"Copperfield's is a very reputable firm, you know," adds Lear smugly. "That's why they employ *me* – best workmanship in London. Lear Eyes are custom made. I can match any human peeper on this earth. Copperfield's takes orders from only the finest of doctors."

They had moved to go, but both stop in their tracks.

"And . . . who would they be?" asks Irene, turning back.

"Mayfair doctors exclusively."

"Much obliged, governor," says Sherlock hastily with a cockney accent, showing the glass blower the top of his head as he lifts his cap. A smile has come over his face.

The store bell tinkles as they leave.

A thick man in a coachman's black livery with two thin red stripes on his coat is standing in the shadows just down Carnaby Street, observing them between pedestrians as they emerge. They are too excited by what they've just learned to notice. They turn up the street, away from the man. A black coach with red fittings awaits him nearby.

"A glass blower on the outskirts of Mayfair who supplies only Mayfair doctors!" Sherlock says into Irene's ear as they walk. He continues to keep his head down for a few strides, then stops. "Our suspect . . . is a man, a wealthy one who almost certainly lives in Mayfair, has brown irises with violet flecks, and a false eye; he not only knew Lillie Irving, but was her secret friend. She lived in Aldgate and was raised in Whitechapel."

Much of it makes sense to Irene – she has followed nearly all of Sherlock's moves. But when she hears him say all he now knows in one categorical sentence, adding things he has learned on his own, it amazes her. Her gloved hand reaches down and takes one of his, with its long, white fingers lined by dirt, and squeezes it. A strange expression comes over his face, a look of wonder, a sudden loss of the haunted, desperate expression he usually wears. Then she lets him go.

She has to get home. Her father will be back soon.

Sherlock is tempted to think about Irene and nothing else for a long time that day – she fascinates him, the most intriguing person he has ever met – but other subjects are competing for attention in the compartments of his brain.

The pieces of his puzzle are being located at an increasing pace. He is putting them into position and setting up the blueprint into which the remaining ones will fit.

The next piece is going to be found on the streets that night. He needs a place to hide. . . . Malefactor's answers are due.

But another subject worries him much more, more than anything he has contemplated since the moment he saw that first article in *The Illustrated Police News.*

He is about to make his mother a part of this deadly game.

15

A DANGEROUS MOVE

The first thing to do that night is locate Malefactor. Sherlock doesn't want to try in the light of day – too risky. The police will be watching. But he has to find him. He needs a report on whatever interviews the Irregulars have conducted in Whitechapel.

He hides in alleys throughout the rest of the day, but as it wears on, becomes restless. He begins to walk aimlessly, his hat pulled down. It seems like there are Bobbies on every street corner and they all appear to be looking for him.

Past midnight he begins searching the streets in earnest. For a while, it feels like the gang has vanished. They don't seem to be in any of the most likely places. He goes farther east than their usual territory and searches near the river. Finally, just past the stone arches of London Bridge, the Tower looming up ahead, he looks toward the east side of the big wharf and sees dark shapes near the old Billingsgate Fish Market. They vanish into the shadows as he approaches, just as they should.

As he nears, the stench of fish is almost overwhelming. Nearby, the brown Thames laps gently. He puts his hand to his nose, turns off the street and walks between a dark warehouse and the big market building, toward the water, his eyes alert. It would be dangerous here even if he weren't a fugitive. During the day it is jammed with people; the vilest words in all of London fill the air. Billingsgate and cursing go together like twins. But at this hour, everything is eerily still. Some of the fishmongers' stalls and sheds stand vacant on the far side of the market, facing the water. Sherlock peers into the crude open stands, looking for the shapes he spotted from a distance. They seem to have disappeared somewhere into this slimy labyrinth. There is a sudden movement behind him.

"Master Sherlock Holmes, I perceive."

Sherlock turns.

The other boy is standing as straight as a statue, legs wide apart and hands on hips, the river behind him.

"Malefactor."

"The one and only." The boss swaggers forward a few steps, apparently unaffected by the chilly late April breeze blowing off the river and the drizzle that is resuming again. "I'm glad you didn't bring the girl. At least you have some sense. This isn't a place for her."

"Nor you, really."

"Not our territory, no."

"Then why?"

"Need you ask?" sneers Malefactor. He points a long bony finger to the north-east. "Whitechapel. We are here, thanks to you. We have made the enquiries. I thought it best for us to be in unexpected places for a day or two."

"Wise."

Malefactor bows slightly.

"And what was the word?" demands Holmes.

The criminal isn't pleased with the way the question is phrased and thinks he detects a slight smile. He doesn't answer. Instead, he asks Sherlock what else he has learned about the murder. The boy reveals a few things, keeps others to himself, and it appears to satisfy. Malefactor finally begins to unveil his answers.

"This is strictly for the girl. Your cause must have some worth to it, if she is interested. There is a villain not playing by the rules here. Our inquiries confirm as much."

Malefactor enjoys keeping his listener in suspense. He adjusts his dirty black topper, this time tipping it back on his domed forehead, smoothes out his tail-coat, and looks at his chewed fingernails.

"There were two screams," he says calmly, "a woman's and then a man's. Several people swear to it. There was a gentleman of wealth rushing from the area, clutching his face. He entered a private coach: black, red fittings. It left at a gallop."

Sherlock is seeing it . . . from above.

"And something else," boasts the young boss.

"The cry of crows," murmurs Holmes.

Malefactor is displeased. It appears as if he wants to strike the other boy again. "Yes," he mutters. His eyes narrow. He doesn't want to say anything more. But he gives in.

"I shan't ask you how you know that. Though I *will* tell you to be careful. Not for your sake, God knows, but for the girl. The sort of person who did this will have the means to make you – and Miss Doyle – vanish. You don't matter to him. Neither did the woman he murdered. That's the way of the world. Get that into your head." Malefactor is almost snarling.

"Which way did the coach go?" inquires Sherlock, gambling that pride will make his rival say even more.

The boy in the top hat shows his teeth. "Think I might not have that answer?"

"I . . . "

"The coach fled from there going west!" Malefactor places his arms across his chest and sticks out his chin, observing Sherlock's reaction.

"Thank y –."

"There is nothing good in this world, but if there were, Miss Doyle would be the closest thing to it. Protect her, or feel my wrath."

"Of cours –"

"Goodnight, Jew-boy."

Malefactor's inquiries have confirmed everything Sherlock has suspected and much more: screams, evidence that the victim saw her attacker, the crows, a rich man fleeing west-ward in a well-described coach . . . west toward Mayfair.

He knows what he has to do next. He has to stride right into the middle of this battle and begin with his dangerous move. He has to involve his mother. She will be giving lessons in rich Mayfair homes this very week.

His parents know he is alive and still in London. They could not have missed the crow he drew on their table.

But he isn't coming tonight to set their minds at rest.

It is early morning and pitch-black in much of Southwark. The freakish people on the streets pass without his notice. He slithers silently through the warrens and cobblestone lanes and soon is near his home. There is the hatter's shop. No one appears to be watching tonight, at least that he can tell. Their little window is dark.

He sneaks along the alley at the back and up the stairs. He lifts the latch. Open.

Again he hears the sounds of his parents sleeping. Crawling across the main room, he stops at his bed. It is empty. He'll have to go straight to their room. There is no door there, just a drape hanging in the entrance. When his face touches it, he can smell her perfume. Though his father doesn't always have tobacco for his stempipe, its aroma is often in their flat. It hangs in the air in the bedroom. Sherlock stops moving. They smell safe. He feels another overpowering desire to crawl into their bed and snuggle between them.

It is strange to see them lying there. They are stripped to their undergarments, wrapped in each other's arms in a deep sleep: he on his back gently snoring, she in her shift with her hand on his chest. It is embarrassing to catch them like this. It isn't what a son is supposed to see. But it nearly makes him cry. He can feel their love and knows it is the best thing on God's earth.

It is time to set aside these feelings. If he doesn't act immediately, he won't act at all. He reaches out and gently places his hand over Rose's mouth. Her eyes fly open. He presses his hand down firmly. She can't scream.

His mother seizes his hand and opens her mouth to sink her teeth into his flesh. Rose Holmes has long since learned how to defend herself.

"Mother!" he whispers as loudly as he dares.

The eyes turn toward him, at first thrilled, then filling with tears. He removes his hand and she sits up in bed, enfolding him in her arms.

"My boy," she whimpers, kissing him.

Beside her, Wilber stirs. He looks up at his son as if he's seeing Marley's ghost and reaches for his wire reading spectacles.

"Sherlock?"

For an instant, the boy thinks his father is going to cry too. Instead, his arms go around his wife. He extends a hand.

"Wonderful to see you, son."

Minutes later they are having cold tea at their little table, using just one candle for light, speaking in hushed tones. Sherlock explains everything that has happened: about his escape, about Irene, Malefactor, the eyeball, Mayfair, and all the evidence he has gathered, even about smelly old John Stuart Mill, which makes his mother laugh. When the tea is done, they pull their chairs close together and are silent. They know that Sherlock can't stay long. They extinguish the candle and huddle in the dark. No one moves, as if they all hope they can forget reality and fall asleep together. Only Wilber, who is given to dozing off, succumbs to the darkness. Rose turns to Sherlock and smiles, motioning toward her husband.

But her son isn't smiling back. His expression has grown serious. Their faces are close enough that she knows, even in the darkness, that he is anxious to tell her something.

"Mother?" he asks in a faint voice.

"Yes, dear?"

"You have to help me."

His voice sounds so somber that she doesn't respond.

"Mayfair is a world unto itself," he continues, as if he needs to explain this clearly. "Everyone is connected to everyone else there."

"I know," says Rose, patting his hand.

"The answer to all of this is inside that neighborhood . . . where you give lessons."

She is beginning to understand what he wants.

"Have you ever seen a man with a glass eye in a Mayfair home?"

"No, though I doubt any gentleman would advertise the fact that he has a false eye, especially to the likes of me." She smiles in an attempt to make light of her comment, showing an echo of the spirit she once had. Sherlock needs her old courage now.

"Could you . . . " he begins.

"Yes, I could," she says, without flinching.

"I can't go there."

"I know." She takes one of his hands into both of hers.

Now that his mother has agreed, Sherlock wants to run away. He shouldn't be doing this.

"No," he says decisively, getting to his feet, regretting that he came here. "You can't be involved in this. It's too dangerous."

She pulls him back down.

"If you are in jail for much of your life, if they . . . hang you, Sherlock, I would never forgive myself for not trying to help. My life would be over anyway."

He pauses for a long time before speaking again.

"Just observe. Look around carefully. That's all. I don't want you to ask anyone anything directly. You might be in the murderer's home or a friend's. We are expendable to people like that. He will be suspicious of any interest in his glass eye from an outside inquirer."

"I will be careful," she assures him, squeezing his fingers.

"You must be."

"But what if I ask a discreet question, something *in*direct? Perhaps of a servant who knows the neighborhood well, who wouldn't normally talk to her master anyway, a scullery maid?"

Sherlock hesitates. "Only if you are absolutely certain about her," he says with emotion, a little louder than he intends.

"What was that?" mutters his father as he comes awake. "Sherlock? What are you two talking about?"

"The physics of flight in the yellow-bellied sapsucker, my dear," smiles Rose.

Humor is not Wilber's strong suit and for a moment, before he laughs, he is a little mystified.

\

No one has to call Sherlock "Judas" now. He's heard the Christian Bible story of that reviled man's betrayal many times in school, and as he works his way through the dark avenues back to Montague Street, he indeed feels like a traitor. Has he gone too far, put his mother in danger – into a situation that might turn her over to the villain? She will be a spy behind enemy lines. If spies are caught, they are executed.

The sun is still a few hours from rising when Sherlock crosses back over the Thames. He doesn't pay much attention to his surroundings, doesn't even try to imitate the street-boy shamble he has perfected. He is too deep in thought. He moves down Montague, under the gaslights, beside the long pale exterior of the British Museum without even glancing behind. The Doyle home is still. He hopes that fleabag J.S. Mill will be indoors tonight. Sherlock slides down the passageway and into the backyard.

A dark object is hanging from the kennel. He can't tell what it is. He moves closer.

It's a bird . . . a large *black* bird. *And it's dead.*

It is attached to the boards just above the entrance. A long-bladed knife has pierced the crow through its breast, pinning it to the wood. Its beak is open as if in a scream. Written just above its shotgun-sprayed little head, in scarlet slashes of blood, are two words. His stomach feels sick as he brings his face within a few wingspans:

Beware Jew!

Sherlock almost cries out. Who, other than the police, could know that he is after the villain? Who is watching him? *Why?* As his eyes dart around the yard, a ghost-like figure comes to mind, one he thought he had imagined – the big coachman in black livery and red standing in the alley observing him and then looking up at the crows. There's an instant connection in the boy's thoughts between that phantom coachman in black . . . and a black coach racing west from the murder! Then he remembers a dark vehicle parked alone on Whitechapel too, on the night he ran from there in fear.

He wipes the scarlet words from the kennel with a quivering hand, leaving a smear of blood. He looks left, right, up above, toward the house, down the passageway. He spots no dark figure. His whole body is shaking. He pulls the blade from the crow's chest, allowing the bird to fall to the ground, then kicks it into the rose bushes and flings the bloody knife after it.

He darts into the passageway and starts to run. But halfway down Montague Street he turns around, sprints back and slips down the passage into the yard. He checks the back door . . . locked. He rushes around to the front and tests it . . . locked. Thank God.

Then he disappears into the wicked London night.

16

THE DEVIL'S CARRIAGE

Sherlock lies on cold, hard cobblestones in a lane behind a pile of rotting vegetables north of the University College of London for several dark hours. He knows he must retreat to an area he doesn't frequent. When the rain pours down, he presses as close to the building as he can get.

Who is that coachman? What has he seen and what does he know? Was he at the Haymarket Theatre too, the glass maker's shop in Soho, following him from the moment he visited the crime scene? *Only the murderer or someone who works for him would do this.* It is obvious. The villain is on to Sherlock . . . and in a murderous mood.

After the sun rises, he makes his way back toward Irene's house, not because he needs food – he'll beg or steal it now – but because he has to see her, warn her, tell her that their meetings will have to be rare, if they take place at all.

He finds a place on the grounds of the British Museum, against the east side of the building inside the wrought-iron fence, where he can see the house and not be detected. He waits. He is frantic. His hands are clammy, his eyes shift in his head, and he holds his spine tightly against the wall. Finally, Andrew Doyle emerges and marches down the street, walking stick in hand.

Sherlock slips across the road and floats down the passageway. Irene is standing in front of the empty dog kennel in a long white dress, staring at the smear of blood, sobbing.

She turns when he comes close. "You're alive!"

Her reddened eyes look big and he thinks she is going to hug him. She advances but stops before they touch.

"When I saw the blood and the empty kennel, I . . . "

"It's crow's blood."

"Crow's?"

"We are in trouble, Irene, enormous trouble," his voice is cracking. "When I got here early this morning, there was a dead crow on the kennel, fastened to it with a knife." He says nothing about the scarlet message.

Irene looks like she might faint. He reaches out and grips her forearm.

"Someone knows what we are doing, someone who will do anything to stop us. Everything has changed. You cannot be part of this now."

"Yes I can," she says, wiping a tear from her cheek. Her face is defiant and her eyes challenge his.

He pauses. He knew it would be like this with Irene Doyle. He'll have to compromise.

"I can't stay here, that's certain," he insists. "And your role *has* to be different. I need to think about how you . . . might still help. In the meantime, stay indoors with the locks bolted when you are alone, keep your eyes open, and you'll hear from me."

Sherlock turns and walks down the passageway.

"Where are you going?" she asks.

A desperate fiend is trying to scare them off. *A killer.* Sherlock has been thinking about whom else might be attacked. And it terrifies him.

"*Where are you going?*" she repeats.

"To warn my parents," he murmurs and walks faster.

This time he makes a beeline for Blackfriar's Bridge. At busy High Holborn he swings east, mixing in with the crowds on their way to work. Everyone is under suspicion now, every man who passes: everyone in front and behind. It is a horrible feeling. A shadow is after him . . . perhaps in other clothing now, watching his movements this very moment. Even the poor little crossing sweepers, who, for pennies, sweep grime and dust from the paths of their betters, appear to be spying. Every look seems to interrogate him, every unusual noise makes him jump. He wishes he could fly above it all and spot his enemies from the air like an eagle. Up Holborn Hill he goes to the teeming place where Gray's Inn Road meets the main street. The crowds are even thicker here. Signs over shops and billboards and posted bills on walls are bigger and more colorful. The traffic of horses and carriages is loud and foul. Sherlock listens to that famous London clamor, then begins to cross the street, moving carefully through the flow.

Something makes him turn.

It is the crack of a whip, the "Hee-ah!" of a carriage driver inciting a team of horses. The vehicle bursts out of the traffic as if its pulling beasts are runaways. It comes in Sherlock's direction, right at him.

That is when he sees Irene.

She is crossing the street too, but behind him: between him and the oncoming carriage. She'd been on the footpath when the driver cracked his whip, too close to the noise of the pedestrians to distinguish the sound of the onrushing coach in the din, and not as alert as she should have been. There had been a brief gap in the traffic: she had darted out, moving as fast as she could in her white dress, her blonde hair shining in the spring sun, her brown eyes watching Sherlock, intent on catching up to him.

"IRENE!" he cries.

Everyone near him seems to turn, like a crowd coming to a halt in a scene from an opera.

The dark coach is bearing down on her, the horses foaming at the mouth as they feel the sharp snaps of the whip. The driver is a big man, leaning forward in his seat, clutching the reins, shoulders as wide as a rugby player's, a black hat pulled down on his forehead, face hidden in a scarf, dressed in *black livery with red stripes* . . . riding a *black vehicle with red fittings*. This is no ghost.

"IRENE!" Sherlock shouts again and runs toward her.

Her mind isn't on the sounds behind her. At first she smiles at the boy as if she were giving in to being spotted. But sensing the panic in his voice, she turns and looks back.

The coach is almost on top of her. She screams and holds out her arms.

Sherlock's long legs take him down the street as if he were flying. He moves like a falcon, directly toward the carriage, sailing right into it. Irene cringes in horror between the boy and the vehicle.

He can almost feel the hot breath of the thundering horses as he extends a hand and seizes the back of her dress between the shoulder blades. He careers to the side, dragging her with him . . . and the coach shoots past.

Saved!

But not quite: her long, white dress flows behind as he snatches her. Fluttering there as if suspended in time, it catches in the spokes of a rear wheel!

Suddenly she is snapped from his grip, pulled like a rag doll back into the street, sucked under the iron wheel, dragged along the hard pavement, and devoured by the machine. Her scream rings in his ears. Blood splatters across the white fabric.

The coach shoots through the traffic and disappears. Everything stops. Sherlock stands still in that moment, his mouth wide open, his eyes cast down the street where the vehicle has spit her out, where she lies in a heap as still as death.

At first he walks slowly. He can't run, doesn't have strength left in his limbs. It is as if this is one of those nightmares in which he can't get to where he is going, and what he is after fades as he struggles to reach it.

Then everything comes back. The sound returns in a rush, time speeds up and he is running, crying out to Irene, his only friend.

But just as he nears her, he sees the first policeman, then another, then another, rushing to the scene. Sherlock halts as if a door has been slammed in his face. He turns and slips into the crowd.

Minutes later he is behind the pillars of an old bank a few streets away, standing in the shadows, ashamed and distraught, crying like he has never cried before.

17

NEW MORNING

He has nowhere to go. Nothing he can do. He can't even speak with his parents. The extreme danger involved in his being anywhere near them now is obvious. He slips away to last night's hiding place in that little lane near the rotting vegetables. Later he moves a few alleys farther north, props himself up against the gray stone wall of a building behind a broken-down horse trough and just sits there. All day, he stares off into space, his eyes red and his brain numb. He can't think anymore.

A sharp pain in his side wakes him in the morning. Malefactor is standing over him, instructing Grimsby.

"Kick him again!" comes the order.

The little thug winds up for another boot to the ribs. Sherlock sees this one coming, but doesn't flinch. Why should he? What is there to live or die for? He doesn't care if Malefactor has him beaten to death right where he lies.

"Cease!" cries the gang leader, holding his walking stick high. The hard boot stops in midair. Grimsby looks disappointed and so does his general. A beating isn't worthwhile if Holmes won't resist.

"Don't you have the self-respect to fight back?" asks Malefactor.

Sherlock merely sits up against the wall, rubbing his ribs. Malefactor kneels down and brings his face up close.

"You did not protect her!" he shouts, his yellow teeth flashing. He looks angrier than Sherlock has ever seen him. "You nearly killed my –" he stops himself, "an angel!"

Nearly?

Sherlock bounces to his feet.

"She's alive?" he cries, returning Malefactor's gaze.

"In the St. Bart's 'ospital, she is, but . . . " pipes up a small Irregular.

Malefactor swings around and whacks the little boy across the mouth with his walking stick. The lad howls and shrinks away. The leader whirls back on Holmes.

"That is not the point! Your guardianship of Miss Irene Doyle was irresponsible and inadequate. I do not . . . "

But Sherlock is gone. Grimsby and Crew find themselves on the ground, knocked backwards, as the tall, thin boy darts through the encircled gang and flies away.

"Come back here!" bellows Malefactor. "Irregulars! Seize him!" But it is too late. The race is won before it begins.

St. Bartholomew's is the oldest hospital in London, there in one form or another for more than seven hundred years.

Sherlock runs until he is out of breath, until the sprawling ancient brick building comes into view beside the Smithfield Market. It is gathered around several blocks, with courtyards in the middle. There are many entrances. Sherlock goes past the main ones and selects a small door in a dark medieval archway. He doesn't need to summon the courage to be here in plain view. He has to see Irene.

He has never been in a hospital before. They are mostly for the working classes, but not for the very poor, not for street people. Perhaps the nurses will throw him out. He's splashed some water from a public pump over his face and rubbed the black off, tried to comb his torn hair with his hands, taken off his cap, stood up as straight as he can. But he is worried he won't be allowed in the building for long.

Irene's stay here will be brief. She was brought to a hospital because she was alone and unconscious; because it was a sudden and severe accident. Otherwise, she would have been taken back to Montague Street. People like Irene Doyle usually convalesce at home with physicians attending them around the clock.

Where will she be in the big building? He enters and rushes past the open door of a cavernous outpatient room with distraught folks sitting on wooden benches under an arched ceiling. Then he slips up a wide, stone stairway. He passes rooms for hospital matrons, others for students, chemical laboratories, physicians' offices, and dun-colored doors with "Sister This-and-That" painted in clear letters.

He tries to look like he has a purpose for being in these high, wide halls with the whitewashed walls. Everything smells clean. But he's heard hospitals breed disease.

Maids move past him carrying mops, and nurses come by in uniforms bearing bottles of medicines. A few summon slight smiles, others questioning looks. Sweeping by big rooms, Sherlock sees rows of patients in beds, some lying still, others moaning. Outright cries of pain echo from other floors.

It suddenly occurs to him that he might be acting rashly. All Malefactor had said was that Irene was alive. Maybe she is unconscious, clinging to life? Maybe she is disfigured, crippled, unable to walk.

ACCIDENT WARD reads a sign over the big double doors of a wing. He enters, and from the hall, sees her in the third room. She isn't moving, her blonde hair spread out around her on the pillow. There are flowers beside her, evidence that her father has been to visit and will soon be back. He has to act quickly.

He tiptoes into the big room, feeling afraid. The other patients appear to be asleep.

"Irene?" he whispers, without expecting a response. But one comes.

"Sherlock?" she asks in a faint voice, her half-open eyes searching for him.

His heart leaps. But what he sees almost makes him turn away. Both her eyes are blackened, there are cuts and bumps on her face, gauze on her lip, and her left arm, resting across her stomach, is heavily bandaged.

She tries to lift her head and force a smile. It looks terribly painful.

"Don't move," he says.

"I'm all right."

"I'm sorry."

"For what?"

"For doing this to you."

"You? The murderer did this, not you. And we're going to catch him."

The words on the chart above her bed read: "mild brain trauma, bruised right cheekbone, fractured left humerus, fractured left metacarpal, cracked 3rd right rib." Sherlock swallows.

Irene isn't going to catch the villain. She isn't going to have *anything* to do with him. Not now. Not ever.

He stands above her, not listening as she speaks. She is planning what they should do next, what he might investigate while she recovers.

"My father thinks it was an accident."

Staring down at Irene's battered face, he feels tears welling in his eyes.

He interrupts her.

"I think I should go."

"Pardon me?" she asks, taken aback, trying to turn her head to see him better.

"I should go. I'm sorry for this. This will never happen again. *Ever.*"

"Sherlock? . . . What are you . . . ?"

But he is gone out the door. The tears are flowing now, rolling down his cheeks. He grinds at his face to wipe them away, rubbing his smelly coat sleeve into his skin until it turns red.

He has brought Irene into a desperate world, one of murder and hatred and greed. It was wrong. Malefactor was right. It isn't a place for her. It is for people like the killer, the Irregulars . . . and Sherlock Holmes.

I hope I never see her again, he tells himself as he hurries down the stairs. He stops at the little door where he entered and straightens up, willing his sadness away and replacing it with anger. If he has to reject the only friend he's ever had, the only one he will *ever* have . . . that is what he will do! Cold, hard reason will be his guide from this moment forward.

Sherlock flings the door open.

Ten strides later he is lying on the cobblestones in the big square in front of the Smithfield Market. Someone has seized him in a wrestler's death grip, both rough fists under his chin, a face within an inch of his.

Malefactor.

He has grabbed Sherlock as if he wants to murder him.

"I knew you'd come here, Jew-boy! I'm warning you. Leave her alone, and leave all this alone! You've done enough damage. You don't know this world. You'll kill more with your meddling. Whoever attacked Miss Doyle will know that you speak to *us!* Go back to the hole you crawled out of and stay there!"

He lifts Sherlock and rushes him into an alley, out of the view of passersby. There he throws him into a wooden rain barrel, bowling it over like a cricket wicket. Malefactor walks up and stands over the boy, taking off his hat and coat, and handing them and his walking stick to Crew.

"I should have done this long ago," he growls. "I shall teach you a lesson!" The Irregulars stand around them with grins on their faces, anxious for the beating to begin.

"Kill 'im!" shouts Grimsby, and it seems like it is going to happen.

But Sherlock shocks them. He isn't one tiny bit afraid now. Instead, his blood is boiling. Kill *him*? Not likely. Not anymore.

Malefactor expects him to curl up into a ball, or if he actually fights back, to stand up and raise his fists.

But Sherlock lashes out from the ground, swinging his long legs around like the blades in a field mower, spinning them powerfully, taking the older boy's pins right out from under him. Malefactor lands in a heap, hard on the ground, a look of utter astonishment on his face. Then Sherlock is after him. He piles on and drives his fists into the criminal's stomach, his face, his throat, between his legs. When fighting the devil, any way of fighting is just.

But when the others pull him off, the strangest thing happens. Malefactor looks at him and laughs.

"Why, Master Holmes, I do believe you have some spunk!" There is blood around his mouth.

"If I had my way, you would get what you *deserve*!" Sherlock screams, unconcerned about who hears. "And everyone who ever hurt anybody in this world would get the same!" The Irregulars are struggling to hold him.

"Ah, an idealist. Stamp out all evil worldwide? Utopia! A noble goal, Master Holmes." His face turns angry. "For an idiot!"

"I'll catch the murderer! You'll see!" spits Sherlock, still straining to get at him.

"The Arab's trial is in ten days, Holmes. Let him die. We live in an evil world. That is the way it is. I have made my peace with it. You should make yours. Justice is a fiction. Let this be!"

"I *know* I can't change the world . . . you fool! But I can change *this!*" rages Sherlock. "I will find the person who killed that woman and whoever hurt Irene. You can make a scurrilous wager on it, and win yourself some coins. That would make you happy. Money always does, doesn't it, every pinch of it that you steal?"

With that, he makes a sudden move and breaks free from the Irregulars. His strength, when summoned, surprises him. He takes two steps toward Malefactor, then stops . . . the crime boss's tall hat is still in Crew's hand. Sherlock kicks it from his grasp and sends it flying across the alley. Then he walks backwards toward the Smithfield Market eyeing his foe, not certain that the gang leader won't attack him from behind.

"This isn't over!" shouts Malefactor as Holmes turns the corner and vanishes into the crowds. Sherlock has a strange feeling . . . that his opponent has a smile on his face.

On his own on the street, his brain is on fire. He tries to calm himself, to think clearly and dispassionately, just as his father taught him. But it is difficult. He is absolutely enraged. He has lost his only friend. He has caused her immense pain. His hatred of the murderer is a seething cauldron inside him.

He will live on the streets from this day on and do anything . . . *anything* . . . to solve this crime. He is going to enter Malefactor's world. Whether it is a place he can survive in or not, he will go there. He will be like those people, do what they do. He will free himself and Mohammad Adalji.

Sherlock will have to wait a few days to hear from his mother about Mayfair, but then he will go straight after his target. There will be no more caution. He won't allow himself such weakness. He has just ten days.

He slips into the shadows. He'll have to steal to endure, sleep in alleys, and avoid the police. But it will all be worth it.

His mother will find something, he is sure. Then he will flush out this fiend! He is certain now that he has the courage to do it.

18

THE WILD SIDE

Two days later, Sherlock goes looking for his mother.

She teaches wherever she is hired in London, and Mayfair girls are her most frequent students this time of year. The "fashionable season" is about to begin: the upper class is moving from their country estates into city homes for the summer. If the villain lives in Mayfair, he will be there now.

Sherlock can't speak to Rose near their home, so he sets out to find her elsewhere.

He imagines what route she might take from Mayfair to Southwark. He knows she often leaves for home about the time he flees Trafalgar, about five o'clock, and guesses she will walk through the Square hoping to catch a glimpse of him.

As the yellow fog grows thicker that day, he cases the narrow streets she might take, keeping his cap tugged down low and hiding among the flowing crowds. Almost as if on schedule, not long after Big Ben chimes 5:00, he sees her. She emerges magically out of the fog, a light in the brown mass of pedestrians. She is moving down the other side of a street in Soho, keeping under the shop canopies, not far from Lear the glassblower's place, looking warily at people as she walks. She appears grayer and tired.

He crosses the street behind her and pursues. Keeping inconspicuous, he dodges through the crowd until he catches up. Passing by, he gently bumps her and murmurs into her ear.

"It's me."

Sherlock moves on, knowing she will follow.

He leads her through the back streets and then into the alleyway behind the Haymarket Theatre. It's a perfect place. When it seems they are alone, she takes him into her arms and doesn't want to let go. "You are in *such* danger," she whispers. He doesn't always respond to her affections, but can't help himself this time. He hugs her too, and waits.

When she pushes him gently back and looks into his eyes, there are tears streaked on her cheeks and her lip is trembling. But he has to be dispassionate, to the point – he has to ask her now, because there is no time to waste.

"Do you have news from Mayfair?"

She can't speak: just shakes her head.

His heart sinks. But then he upbraids himself. He knows what he has to do.

"I think I can solve this, mother," he says, hoping he can convince her.

"I pray you can, Sherlock, but . . . "

"I can, praying or not."

"But how? You are just . . . "

"I need you to be *brave*," he says with feeling, empha-
sizing the last word.

It takes her a while to realize what he means. For a
moment she seems to hesitate, but then nods.

"I'll make direct inquiries."

Sherlock's voice quavers as he responds. "Never to the
gentleman of the house, never to his wife, his family, his
footman . . . or his coachman especially. Be very careful . . . "

"Direct inquires. I will find people to ask. That's
what I'll do," she insists in a strong voice, summoning her
courage once more, the kind she'd had in the days when she
defied her parents.

They leave the alleyway separately, Rose trying to keep
that steely resolve, Sherlock working hard to prevent his
feelings of guilt from overwhelming him.

"I'll find you in four days," are his last words to her.
He tells her nothing about the attack on Irene.

There is little more Sherlock can do while he waits. He
has his hands full just avoiding all his pursuers: the police,
and the villain and whoever might work for him. Steering
clear of the first isn't his most difficult challenge. At least he
knows what the Bobbies and most detectives look like, and
where they tend to be. But eluding the other threat gives him
constant terror. He expects an attack at any moment. He
keeps changing his appearance, trading coats and hats with
other street people, frequenting different parts of the city.

Each night he sleeps in a new alleyway – the second night he walks far out of the city and makes his bed in long grass next to a stone fence in a pasture. And all the while he thinks of his parents and prays they are safe . . . especially his mother.

Mohammad Adalji has similar prayers. In his cell on Bow Street he thinks of his mother and father, who both went back to Egypt last year. They don't even know he is in jail. At night when he dreams, it is of hot Cairo skies and the happy games he played with his friends. But he sleeps lightly and awakens at the slightest sound . . . clutching at his neck whenever a door slams. He knows it is inevitable now . . . his death is fast approaching. There's one week left.

Sherlock needs to keep himself fed. He must have better food than he can get from stealing little crusts of bread from the pigeons at Trafalgar. But he has to do it without making a scene. He has to be sly and invisible, use his magical skills of observation.

The best place to perform his wizardry is at the Smithfield. The city is full of markets but this one has two advantages. It is well placed, close to where he wants to be, but not too close, and it is big and always massed with people.

At first he survives on rotting food plucked after hours from near-empty carts. All the while he cases the market with attention to detail and resists doing more. The meat that is sold inside the new, glass-covered, brick building that stretches for several blocks, doesn't interest him. What can he do with cuts of cow cheeks and ox hearts, or skinned rabbits hanging from hooks? His target is the busy outdoor market where shoppers move shoulder-to-shoulder in pursuit of deals. Food stalls line both sides of artificial avenues, fed by hordes of loaded barrows: two-wheeled carts filled with vegetables, fruit, and eggs. It is as if the food is waiting for Sherlock, laid out but guarded by barrow boys.

Holmes examines the customers who frequent the market, observes the habits of the vendors, and watches anyone who might be watching him, observing like a hovering crow.

Within two days he has picked out a menu of potential victims and then whittled it down to a few. His attention is trained on the servants of wealthy families (from whom he can steal without feeling guilty). He can tell the relative fortunes of their employees by their clothing and the softness of their hands – by their bearing. He soon observes that many have habits. Buyers like to muse over the items for sale, choose them and set them down in their baskets while they pay. Many place the food in front of them; others rest the produce on the pavement, wedging it between their feet and the stall, keeping it safe.

But one woman does it differently. Sherlock picks her out and watches closely. He can tell she is new to this. She moves up and down the avenues past the stalls many times before she chooses her food. She has a certain self-satisfied look that few lowly servants given the job of buying food at a market assume. This is a higher-paid employee, perhaps the cook herself, selecting provisions for a few days, while a lesser servant is ill, or has been dismissed.

The boy watches everything she does. For two consecutive days she picks out her food and sets her baskets down on the cobblestones in front of the stalls – off to her side, neither foot near it. Then she fumbles in her big pockets for her coins and takes a long time to complete the transaction. Sherlock checks the position of the sun to calculate the time she appears both days.

He sees many other opportunities the third day, but waits for her. He notices a tall Bobbie strolling through the crowds. The boy will have to do this perfectly.

She arrives, right on time. One particular stall has become her favorite. She struggles through the crowd toward it, peeved about being jostled, her head tilted slightly back, looking down her nose at others. Sherlock moves stealthily toward the same stall, following a different route. He has to time it right. He has to get there just as she is putting her goods into her baskets. The Bobbie appears to have headed the other way, though every now and then he looks back.

The woman moves up to the stall. There: half a dozen apples, five or six big potatoes, a few fistfuls of carrots, some watercress, and a plump turnip. Into her two baskets they go. There: she sets them down . . . looks up.

Sherlock checks the Bobbie . . . facing the other way. He swoops. Rushing in, bent over and out of the vendor's sightline, he snatches both brimming baskets.

But another hand, just as low to the ground, reaches out too! Sherlock's heart almost stops. There is no turning back. He either gets away or everything is lost. He shoots into the thick masses like an arrow, rising up as he flies. No one shouts. No one seems to follow. Everything and everyone is swallowed up in the throngs. Glancing back, he glimpses a lad eyeing him while moving like lightning from the stall, but not pursuing. Sherlock remembers now that the hand had been smallish: dirty too, and tipped with mangled fingernails.

He knows the rascal . . . one of the smallest Irregulars, the one Malefactor had cracked in the face with his stick. The boy had let Sherlock go, but not because he had any feelings for him. In this world of deceit and sleight-of-hand, victory is given without complaint to the swiftest and the cleverest of the streets. Malefactor will likely never even hear of it. The boy won't want to upset his general, and losing a prize to Sherlock Holmes would most certainly cause the gang leader to internally combust.

Sherlock has enough to last him a week, but that isn't what pleases him most. He knows he has done things very well indeed – he identified and pursued the same victim as an Irregular . . . and beat a trained thief to the prize.

His brain never stops humming. Sometimes he wishes he could pull a lever and turn it off, but it just keeps spinning.

Walking the streets that week, or even trying to go to sleep at night, he finds himself calculating and imagining. He wonders, for example, about blood.

It must be true that everyone's blood is different. And if so, shouldn't there be some way of identifying strains of blood in a chemical laboratory? Not just blood types, but *individual* blood. Might humanity not make that discovery some day? Couldn't samples of blood, like those splattered on the glass eyeball hidden in J.S. Mill's dog kennel be examined, so that detectives could know to whom it belongs? That blood might not all be Lillie's . . . perhaps some belongs to the villain.

Crouching within his black, oily feathers at the side of the building in the alley near Whitechapel Road, Sherlock sees, in more detail now, the struggle below. Malefactor said there were *two* screams: a woman's *and* a man's . . . and the man ran from the scene, *clutching his face.* Sherlock sees Lillie's mouth contort, hears her scream, sees her rake her attacker's cheek in a dying thrash, plunge a finger into his eye – gauge it from its socket!

There are times when Sherlock despises his own mind, cursed as it is with an imagination as vivid as Mr. Dickens'.

He is ever-vigilant for the dark coachman, but grows more careless about the police, becoming bolder and more curious about their plans as he travels the streets alone. He wonders how aggressively they are pursuing him now. Before long, he is actually following Peelers, eavesdropping when two or more gather in a group, listening to their conversations.

The day before he is supposed to see his mother, he goes too far.

He decides to return to Trafalgar. It is particularly crowded there and he thinks he can take a chance. He expertly trails a Bobbie through the mass of people across the Square toward another constable, and sits down within earshot. As he leans against the base of Nelson's Column they stand in front of him watching the passersby. He is listening intently when he sees both policemen stiffen.

"Sir!" they both say together.

Sherlock turns to see Inspector Lestrade approaching. His head instantly drops to his chest.

"Good day."

"Gentlemen," says a higher voice. It sounds like it comes from a boy. Sherlock peers out from under his cap. It is a lad indeed, the spitting image of Lestrade, except for the mustache. He looks a little older than Sherlock and wears a brown tweed suit.

"This is my son, constables: Lestrade the Second."

They all laugh. But the inspector's boy doesn't.

"Helping Father, are we?" says one of the Peelers once the laughter subsides.

"Yes," comes the dead-serious response. "I intend to follow in his footsteps."

"A detective, no less. And what are you on the lookout for today?"

"A boy whom we once had in custody pertaining to the Whitechapel murder. We know he is about, and know he has a friend who was nearly killed in a traffic accident recently. Eyewitnesses claimed she had a boy with her, but he vanished."

Sherlock's pulse quickens.

"Sherlock Holmes," says the elder Lestrade. "We have our main villain. But there is still the question of the purse."

"Precisely," says the junior detective. "So we shall jail Master Holmes again if we find him, and proceed with prosecution. If you see him, let us know." The policemen nod solemnly. "His friend, this girl, is at home now. She wasn't forthcoming when questioned, but they may try to meet."

Sherlock is petrified. He doesn't dare move. But as the Lestrades turn to go, the younger one walks directly his way! He curls up into a ball.

"Boy," says young Lestrade firmly, reaching into his pocket. In horror, Sherlock realizes that it is he who is being addressed.

"Boy!"

"Yes?" Sherlock offers.

"Do you want this or not?" There is a farthing in his hand.

"It's me eyes, sir . . . " mumbles the beggar. "I'm blind . . . I don't like to look up."

The coin clatters on the pavement in front of him.

"God bless you, sir," says Sherlock Holmes.

Having escaped such a close call, it would make sense to lie low for a while. But the news about Irene is too much to resist. He doesn't want to speak with her, doesn't want her to see him, but maybe, just maybe, *he* might see *her*.

He makes his way up to Montague Street that night, finds his spot in the shadows outside the British Museum and watches the Doyle house. The lights are still on. He can see figures moving inside. It looks warm in there. There is Mr. Doyle . . . and there is Irene. She passes by quickly . . . too quickly. Then she passes again. He waits. Soon she comes to the window and looks out. She seems to be searching the streets. Her left arm is in a sling. It is hard not to stare at her. She is everything that is right about the world in a world that has so much wrong.

He stays there until their lights go out and then slumps to the ground against the wall and can't leave. Eventually his eyelids start to close, but just before he falls asleep, he sees movement outside the house.

The front door is opening and someone is coming out. Whoever it is, he or she is walking slowly, gingerly, as if it is painful to move.

Irene. She's dressed in dark clothes.

He shrinks back against the wall.

She comes out to the street, closes the wrought-iron gate, and turns down the foot pavement. She is heading into the city alone. He can't believe it. All her injuries are to her upper body, but walking must be excruciating.

He follows. If anyone touches her, he will protect her with his life.

The fog is beginning to settle in.

She seems to be looking for someone. *Me?* thinks Sherlock.

Maybe. He follows her into areas he has recently frequented. As he grows more and more anxious for her safety, he draws closer, hidden by the fog.

They are moving along a narrow street when she suddenly tries to pick up the pace. Soon she is almost running, hobbling forward. He can tell by the way she holds her free hand in a fist that she is frightened. Out in front of her, a shadow seems to be scurrying. Then she comes to a halt, her chest heaving, and shouts:

"MALEFACTOR!!"

There is silence. The noise echoes in the narrow street as if all of London has stopped to listen. And then, from the very place where that shadow evaporated, a bigger one appears.

"Miss Doyle, a pleasure to greet you. Please excuse the conduct of my young associate – it is in his nature to flee."

His hat is in his hands. He has flattened down his greasy hair, his yellow teeth are showing, and he wears a genuine smile. Sherlock can't believe that the young master criminal hasn't spotted him, but Malefactor's eyes are fixed on the girl and the fog is heavy. Holmes looks to his side. He is within a yard of a deep doorway. He disappears into it, so close to the others that he can hear every word they say. She has no experience in street whispers and speaks as if she is in a drawing room with one of her father's friends. Malefactor replies, out of respect, in clear tones.

"I . . . I . . . " she begins.

"How are your injuries, my dear?" He seems truly upset. The sight of her in this condition appears to pain him. He holds out his hands as if to touch her, but then folds them into each other in front of his chest.

"My health is returning," she responds and then adds quickly, "I am looking for Sherlock." She speaks as if she has come to say something difficult and is adamant about stating it bluntly.

There is a long pause.

"Master Holmes?" asks the outlaw as he tries to maintain his smile.

"Yes, sir."

"I would prefer that you call me Malefactor, all my friends do."

Irene says nothing. Sherlock peeks out from his spot. She seems to be breathing heavily, as if she is still very frightened.

"You are trembling, Irene. May I call you that? There is nothing to fear. I will not harm you. In fact, you are safer now than you have been for weeks. I shall see you home untouched. That idiot Jew, whom you say you want to find, almost had you killed."

"It was not his fault," she insists, looking down.

"Oh?"

"He is only seeking justice. It is what I seek too."

"Justice? Not justice again!"

"Yes," she says clearly, without flinching.

"Come, come, now. There has never been, is not now, nor will there ever be such a thing as justice." He spits out the last word as if it tastes vile in his mouth.

"I would dispute that."

"If justice were about in our lifetime then my existence would be different from this." He holds his hands out from his body, palms up, and gestures to the surroundings as if he were a king showing off his realm. He lowers them. "The children of London would not be dying in the rookeries." He eyes her and his voice softens. "You and I would not be standing here as we are; we would be equals. . . . forgive me, that is incorrect. No one, my dear, is your equal. And I do not flatter."

Irene blushes and her head lowers.

"But if justice existed, we would at least look each other in the eye. . . . I might take you for a ride about London in my carriage, and we'd promenade in Hyde Park."

"I do not know, sir, what befell you in your life, but I do know that whatever it was, it should not have turned you away from doing what is right."

"I do what is right every day, Irene. That is how I survive."

"Then help me find Sherlock. . . . Help me free him and Mr. Adalji . . . and keep us all from more harm."

"I . . . " Malefactor falters.

"Help us find that woman's murderer."

"I had a sister . . . " He says in a strange voice, then stops and shakes his head as if he were trying to shake something out. He smoothes his black tail-coat and doesn't speak for a while. Then he addresses her sincerely.

"If you give me your hand and ask for help, I will do it. I cannot make any more inquiries. It is not wise. But I can do something. A reasonable request from you will not go unheeded. Ask."

Irene pauses, thinking.

"I will not ask you to find Sherlock," she begins. "Or to pursue this case. But I will ask you this. . . . If he comes to you for help . . . and wants something you *can* provide . . . will you first, not harm him, and secondly, give the advice he seeks?"

Malefactor says nothing. Sherlock peers around the doorframe, trying to see. There are times when he actually feels something like pity for the young crime boss. There is no question that he has suffered a terrible fall, that his parents are gone, a precious sister is dead, that it has all been unfair.

Irene reaches out her hand and takes one of Malefactor's – his rough left hand that has been hanging limp by his side. Her soft, white hand envelops it.

"Yes," he says softly, and Sherlock thinks he can almost hear the other boy swallow.

"He needs you," smiles Irene, "especially now." Then her face grows taut and she takes a deep breath. She has wanted to tell Malefactor this from the moment she saw him tonight. "I . . . had someone take me to Sherlock's home yesterday, hoping he might be nearby. I had the feeling I was being followed. And just as I was leaving, I saw a carriage pull up and stop there for the longest time."

"Perhaps a detective?" asks Malefactor, acting disinterested.

"It was . . . " she shudders and touches her bruised face, " . . . *a black coach with red fittings.*"

Sherlock snaps back his head and knocks his shoulder against the wooden door. Malefactor, a reptile sensing prey, instantly swivels toward him. The criminal pulls his hand from Irene's and glares at the doorway, not more than twenty yards away.

Sherlock has no choice. He tears into the street.

"HOLMES!" he hears Malefactor shout.

Sherlock vanishes into the fog. The heels of his old boots smack against the cobblestones, echoing in the street. He expects to hear the footsteps of a dozen boys in hot pursuit. But there are none. All he senses is Irene's hand, reaching out to grip Malefactor again, holding him to his promise, and the leader's other hand rising to halt his troops, though it frustrates him to do it.

As Sherlock runs, his mind is racing. He *has* to do something . . . *now!* He will see his mother tomorrow.

This deadly game is afoot!

19

THE EYES OF MAYFAIR

Sure that no one had followed or spotted him the last time he intercepted his mother coming home from Mayfair, Sherlock decides it is safe to meet her in the same area again. He slides down Carnaby past Lear's shop, turns at Beak Street, and then walks west, staying close to the buildings. He repeats the route twice before he catches sight of her. Though she looks as if she's aged even more in the last few days, a hint of excitement is mingled with the worry and sadness in her face. Her eyes are shifting back and forth as if she knows Sherlock is nearby. He creeps up behind her and in minutes they are behind the Haymarket again.

The boy has been having second thoughts during the day: perhaps, if he flees the city and tries to start life again somewhere else, the murderer will leave his parents alone. He's been thinking about the black coach sitting outside their home; of it brutally trampling Irene. This has all grown too dangerous.

But then his mother turns to him with shining eyes.

"I've done it!" she gasps.

"Mother, I . . . "

"I have news. News you won't believe."

He hesitates. "You found a one-eyed man?"

"I found four."

Sherlock is speechless.

"And they know each other. I have it straight from a long-serving housemaid." Rose catches her breath. "Do you remember when I told you about the Mayfair gentleman who treated his wife terribly and had a strange look in one of his eyes? How one eye seemed dead?"

Sherlock nods.

"Well, the housemaid I asked was one of his. That gentleman, that brutish Mayfair man . . . has a false eye."

Sherlock still doesn't know what to say. What if they are really on the verge of solving this? What are the chances that there are more than four one-eyed men in wealthy little Mayfair? Isn't one of them almost surely the murderer? He swallows hard. Maybe the nasty one *is* him! He has to stay calm. He is getting ahead of himself. Just because this man is unpleasant, doesn't mean he is the villain. There are three others to consider.

"What do you mean they all know each other?" he asks.

"I was told that they have a great deal in common. All four married up in society; owe their wealth to their wives, bought positions in the army. All four were officers during the Crimean War and had the misfortune to suffer wounds to their eyes. On the first weekday in each month they get together, raise a glass of port, and talk about old times."

A league of one-eyed men.

"And here are their names."

One of Rose's shaking, aging hands plucks a torn piece of paper out of the pocket in her dress. There are four names scrawled on it, and beside them, four addresses.

"Mother, you shouldn't have . . . "

She puts a quivering finger to his lips.

"Don't say another word. I asked more questions, yes, found their addresses. That is what you need. Solve this, son. Free yourself and that poor man, and come home to me. And let that woman rest in peace."

She'd told him what to do.

Staggering through Trafalgar Square, reeling from what she said and not watching for enemies, he considers his options. Fleeing is not one of them. The villain might not know he is gone for some time or might do something to make sure he stays away. He must solve the crime and do it soon. It's the only way to make sure they'll all be safe forever.

"Master 'olmes!" says a voice through cupped hands. He's been spotted. Without thinking, he responds by lifting his head.

He's near Dupin's kiosk. The crippled newspaper vendor is motioning him over.

"'ead down!" he instructs. "What's wrong with you, guvna'? You're about in plain view!"

Sherlock snaps out of his stupor and lowers his head.

"Take this," mutters Dupin and jams something into the boy's grimy coat.

The News of the World.

He leafs through it, his mind riveted elsewhere, knowing he must act immediately, but not sure how. There is little in the paper on the Whitechapel murder, anyway. Mohammad's fate is sealed. In five days, he goes to trial. It will be over in an instant. Sherlock can barely think. What is he going to do? The big daily ad for entertainments at The Crystal Palace looks back at him; beside it a much smaller one for a chimney cleaning company.

Chimney sweeps! He looks down at his frame . . . thin as a rail.

He has to get close to his suspects, *very* close, and he has to find indisputable evidence of one man's guilt. Suddenly . . . he knows how he'll do it.

He crosses the river and walks south for miles out of the city into the new suburbs and on toward the green, rolling pastures and villages of Sydenham. No one seems to be following him. He finds another field, another stone fence, and collapses. It is a beautiful, early May evening and as the sun falls, he can hear the birds singing. Somewhere not far off, crows are calling. He drifts into the deepest sleep he has had for weeks. He is frightened, but his mind is set.

He has come to this countryside in pursuit of the tools he needs to execute his final and most dangerous moves. The Crystal Palace is just a mile or two away; in fact, he saw it glowing in the night when the sun first set. Wilber Holmes works there, and though he may never know it, he is about to become an accomplice in his son's desperate scheme.

When Sherlock wakes, the sun is already well up in the sky. He finds a stream and tries to make himself as respectable as possible, then begins trekking through the fields past the village of Forest Hill and along a road into Sydenham. There, on an elevated stretch of land, sits the mighty Palace.

It was built in 1851 as part of the Empire's Great Exhibition, right near the heart of London in beautiful Hyde Park. Much of the world came to the city that year to see the grandeur of Queen Victoria and her people. From Europe, Asia, Africa, the Far East, and America, an incredible one million per month passed through its doors. Inside, nations (naturally lead by the British Empire) displayed the progress of civilization: spectacular new machines, remarkable weapons, exotic silks, precious china, and famous jewels. It was a magical building made of nearly a million square feet of glass, like a see-through castle from the future come to life.

When the Exhibition ended, its masterminds did another amazing thing. They packed it up and moved it, thousands of tons of iron and glass, to this hill in Sydenham. There "The Palace of the People's Pleasure" grew and show business added its flavor: you could see Blondin on the high rope, The Farinis flying through the air, operas so big they might have been performed for God, circuses with their roaring menageries, and Ethardo, balancing on his ball as he climbed his twisting slide to the sky.

It looms now in front of him.

Sherlock can never decide exactly what it looks like: either the biggest glass cathedral the world has ever known, or a greenhouse made for giants. It stretches an impossible length, its endless panes of curved glass walls and ceilings shine in the sun.

People are moving in crowds from the train stations as he ascends the massive grounds, past the life-size models of ancient dinosaurs, the colorful flowers, and the many pools, artificial lakes, and magnificent fountains.

The boy has been here before on a few free employee days with his parents. He knows exactly where he needs to go and how he needs to do this. He walks up one of the huge stone staircases. The steps lead to a wide, wrought-iron-gate entrance.

In order to get in, he is going to try what the Irregulars call "the rush," a simple way of entering a crowded event without paying. He's heard Malefactor instruct his charges about it before. The rush simply involves getting into the flow of a crowd and moving quickly, eyes looking forward, giving the impression that you are meant to be where you are, walking forthrightly into any venue. If you do it correctly, you will rush past the ticket taker and into the building. If he calls out to you, you never look his way, but simply keep moving and disappear into the entering throng. It works best in wide, crowded entrances, and such is the case today. In Sherlock goes, eyes cast into the Palace, moving spryly with the flowing mass. They sweep him ashore.

The boy doesn't even bother to look up at the magnificent glass ceiling. He has to find his father. At exactly noon each day, Wilber releases the birds.

Sherlock's scheme for getting close to the Mayfair suspects, so close that he can prove one guilty, is a daring, almost reckless plan. He is about to put it in motion.

The moment when his father releases the Palace's doves of peace is always spectacular. Thousands of birds are freed from their cages at once, watched by much of the day's crowd, sometimes numbering more than twenty thousand strong. Sherlock has seen it and loves it. Everything seems to stop when the moment comes. All eyes go to the glass roof as the birds soar. The boy, given to being just as interested in a crowd's reaction as he is in the attraction itself, remembers looking up, and then down at the spectators' awed response. That was when he noticed that even the professionals who had seen the doves fly so many times were riveted. Among them were the dancers who performed the popular Chimney Sweep Stroll not long after. A row of them sat on benches nearby and stood as thousands of white wings took flight. Each had a handbag. Each left it unattended as they looked to the ceiling.

Sherlock is guessing that those bags contained their costumes.

He sees his father at a distance. Wilber is immersed in his job. He has the ability to do that, to set aside whatever trials life has given him and concentrate. Sherlock can see the lines in his face, which seem deeper every year. The boy wishes he could speak with him.

But not today.

He keeps his eye on his father's progress and slips around to where the chimney sweep dancers are gathering. There they are, bags in hand, sitting. He creeps up close, pretending to be fascinated by the preparations for the release of the doves.

He waits.

Noon hour. His father is always punctual. A great fanfare of trumpets begins. The crowd hushes. They watch the cages. The dancers stand up, setting their bags on the floor.

Whooooooooooooosh!

Up go the doves. Up go the eyes of nearly twenty thousand people. Sherlock pounces.

Seconds later he is running across the grounds of the Palace, heading north toward the city, a chimney sweep's handbag in his grip. It is his ticket into the mansions of Mayfair.

But first he will hold Malefactor to the pledge he made to Irene.

It doesn't take Sherlock long to find the Irregulars. They, after all, are keeping an eye out for him. He spots a dirty little head looking his way from a lane near the Seven Dials. It pops back and disappears. Sherlock enters the lane.

Malefactor is leaning against a dirty building, tight-lipped as his rival approaches. The mixture of respect and hatred that is always in his face when they meet has increased. He isn't pleased that he is being compelled to help Sherlock Holmes, that he and Irene were listened to, undetected, that this upstart is doing well. He clearly wants to scream at the boy or strike him, but he can't – his voice and his arms are pinned back by the words of Miss Doyle.

"I need some advice," says Sherlock, stopping just beyond an arm's length away.

Malefactor lunges, seizing him by the shoulders and pulling him down an intersecting passageway and into a little court. There, he pitches him to the ground. An abandoned vendor's basket is overturned nearby. The gang leader picks it up, straightens it, and sits on it, his eyes dead, his mouth closed. Several Irregulars, led by Grimsby and Crew, slither up to listen.

"I knew from the beginning that the Arab didn't do it," snaps the boss. "But you, how did *you* know?" It isn't for Sherlock Holmes to know more about a street murder than he. At the very least, the outlaw wants further information in exchange for his advice.

Sherlock doesn't want to tell his rival. It's never seemed right to him to tell this criminal everything he knows.

"How were you so sure the Arab was innocent?" repeats Malefactor, impatient.

"By looking into his eyes," says Sherlock, sitting up and rubbing an elbow.

"Not good enough, idiot!" screams Malefactor, standing up and looming over him.

The boy needs more from the gang leader – so he will have to play cricket with him.

"Because of what he said about the crows," says Sherlock.

"Yes?" It means Holmes is to say more.

"When I first spoke to him," Sherlock continues, "he mentioned very innocently that he'd seen the crows in the sky at the Old Bailey courthouse. That was *all* he knew about them."

Malefactor grasps it instantly.

"Elementary, Holmes." He nods, "The Arab hadn't seen or heard the crows before, but the *murderer* would have. The person who killed that woman heard the crows scream and saw them in the alley . . . and would *never* forget it."

"I'd just told Mohammad that the crows led me to the murder site."

"And he never made a connection."

"Precisely."

"Simplicity itself," Malefactor mutters.

"You and I think alike sometimes," says Sherlock.

"Not really," retorts the older boy. "You want some advice? . . . Talk."

Holmes gathers himself. "I have to break into a house in Mayfair."

Malefactor wonders what Holmes is getting himself into. "First," he begins, "you need an obvious reason to be there, so that if someone sees you on your way, they won't be suspicious."

"I have a reason. I am a chimney sweep."

He pops open the handbag and pulls out his costume and containers of makeup.

Malefactor raises his eyebrows. He is astonished. Holmes has picked the perfect disguise – one that will allow him to get into a house – black, so as to camouflage him at night, take him down the chimney instead of through a door, and make him unrecognizable if someone sees him.

"You must be in the house for only a brief time. You will know exactly what you are looking for before you enter – and where it is apt to be. Therefore, you will visit the house ahead of time and observe your entry point and how to get to it. You will note the occupants of the house and their habits."

Sherlock nods.

"Either the house will be empty, or everyone will be asleep when you enter. If that does not turn out to be the situation, you will immediately vacate the premises. You will know, at all times, exactly where, and how, you will leave the building."

Malefactor pauses. He motions for the Irregulars to leave, then moves closer to the tall, thin boy.

"What exactly, might I ask, are you looking for?" He knows the boy has been withholding information.

"A one-eyed man."

"And a lady's coin purse?"

"Precisely."

Sherlock chooses the first address on Rose's list, the one where the rude man lives. Then he puts on his chimney sweep costume and enters Mayfair. He's never seen anything like it. This is an opera for the rich. The big, white and yellow houses rise on each side of every street like the ornate homes of gods, many five storeys high: gleaming black iron gates on the streets, pillars up the steps at the arched entrances, flowered balconies on upper floors, and areas for servants below stairs. Ladies with purple parasols and matching silk dresses stroll by or clatter past in phaetons and broughams, attended by liveried coachmen. Butlers and footmen appear on front steps. Uniformed cooks and maids scurry around the houses and in through back doors.

Sherlock's destination takes him into the heart of Mayfair, past the extravagant shops of New Bond, onto a smaller street leading to extra wealthy Berkeley Square, and just past it. He begins casing the house, watching every-thing that happens near it and around it. He notes the help, the lady, the perfectly dressed children . . . and then, just as the sun sets, the gentleman on his way home. He is a big man, broad shouldered and a little fat, his cheeks and chin overgrown with red mustachios and a long, red goatee – indeed the cad whose face his mother disliked, and maybe, just maybe . . . the villain. One eye never blinks.

After the man enters his house, Sherlock looks through one of the tall front windows. From there he can see much of the ground floor – a majestic dining room filled with gleaming furniture. He walks casually down the street and returns, then glances in the other front window and sees a wood-stained staircase leading upstairs.

He's heard that there are never bedrooms on the ground floors of the rich. As dangerous as it is, he will have to enter one. That is where he will find the man himself. Moreover, if there is any evidence of guilt about, it won't be in the areas of the house the rest of the family frequents. Sherlock isn't sure how the rich live, but he has a feeling that unlike his poor mother and father, many wealthy husbands and wives sleep in separate bedrooms, in their own private worlds.

He has to go upstairs, find where the man sleeps or where his desk or study is, where he might keep something he wants to hide from others. If anything incriminating was in the villain's possession when he left the murder scene, Sherlock is betting that it made sense for him to keep it, thinking at first that no one would ever dream of searching a Mayfair mansion, then within a day, knowing that an Arab would swing for the crime and he would never be a suspect. There would be a smarter time to destroy it, after the butcher-boy is dead and the case is closed.

Sherlock looks up at the house. There are five chimneys. He will get in through one of them. He heaves a sigh. It is nearly six o'clock. The whole family is home. The time has almost come.

Tonight!

20

CRIMINAL ACTS

Sherlock appears on the grand street that night like a shadow. He has taken off his shoes and blackened his ankles and the tops of his feet. He moves silently and stealthily, finds a house nearby that is easy to ascend – it has a little lane, and iron rungs on its side for laborers to use when repairing its roof – and in minutes has climbed to the top. He crosses three attached houses, up and down on the slanted surfaces above the top-floor servants' quarters, with barely a sound. His feet pat gently on the tiles.

Soon he is on the one-eyed man's roof.

There are the chimneys. He chooses the largest one, which will take him straight down onto the ground floor of the house.

"In and out quickly," he says to himself.

It isn't difficult to get on top of the brick column, but going down and coming back up will be hell. Just decades ago, most sweeps had been small children; but the climbing boys' treatment had been brutal and exploitive. Now there are age restrictions. But even for the dirty, skeletal older boys and men who hold these jobs, climbing up and down

the barely foot-wide chimneys, like the one Sherlock peers
down now, is a daunting task. He thrusts a hand inside. At
least it isn't hot, no recent fires. Being built like a starving
man is, for once, going to be helpful.

He takes a deep breath and wedges himself in.

It is tight and claustrophobic, so much so that he thinks
he'll soon be squeezed to death or become stuck and then
roasted in the morning. Somehow, he has to move down-
ward. Twisting himself like a contortionist, he descends
inch by inch, skinning his arms, his chest, and his legs. It
seems to take forever. He can't make a sound – he goes
down through the interior of the house, all five storeys, past
sleeping servants, owners, and children. His muscles begin
to ache. He stops once and stares back up at the opening,
wondering how he will ever go back up. Several times, he
fears he'll let go and fall, but finally, he lands safely. *He is
actually inside the house.* His heart beats as though it will
burst from his chest.

He is in the fireplace on the ground floor. In front
of him stands the regal dining-room table, its mahogany
surface covered with a white lace cloth, attended by five
chairs, all carved in rich French style. Silently, he brushes
the extra grime from his rags and the soles of his feet,
removes the fire screen, steps over the grate, and avoids
the coal scuttle. The steady tick of a big clock in the hall
makes the only sound in the house. The long windows
have dark drapes that hang to the floor, paintings cover
the walls, ferns sit in vases, and his bare feet stand on a
soft, ornate green carpet. Gingerly feeling a path around

the table, he finds his way into the hallway. Straight ahead is the morning room, to his left the big staircase, and to his right . . . the front door. Memorize it; the quickest way out in an emergency.

He turns to the stairs and places his feet carefully on the wide wooden steps, minimizing creaks. His legs are shaking, but he does it well and within seconds is on the first floor. He turns down the hallway. A drawing room full of furniture spreads out to the right. *Where is the master's bedroom? Where is his study?*

But he never makes it to either.

Edging down the hall, his breath coming in gasps, his sleeve brushes against a little round table. There is a jingling sound and something starts to fall. Frightened, he throws a hand out and catches it.

Sherlock stands stock still for a full minute, waiting to hear the sound of the house rousing, remembering the route down the stairs and out the front door.

But no one stirs.

What does he hold in his hand? It is a wooden container of some sort, the size of a snuffbox. Slowly, he opens it and slides his hand inside. It is a small ball . . . made of glass.

When Irene searched the directories at the library she had also checked for information about glass eyes. Though she hadn't found much, she did learn the simple fact that they sometimes become cracked or nicked . . . and most people keep extras.

Has Lady Luck smiled on Sherlock tonight?

He kneels on the floor and pulls a match from his pocket, an essential tool of a thief. Malefactor had roughly thrust a few into his hand as they departed that afternoon.

He lights it. He'll only have a second and then the flame and its smoke will have to be extinguished.

There is the eyeball with its . . . pale blue iris.

It takes him an excruciating amount of time to get back up the chimney and onto the roof. It is a harder climb than he even imagined – several times he thinks he won't make it. But he has to, so he does. Battered and bruised, blood on his rags, he actually smiles when he reaches the roof – he knows all he needs to know about this house and its owner. This gentleman is not his villain.

It is one of the other three.

He wants to keep moving quickly. Maybe that is careless, but he fears that the villain's side may strike at any moment. The next morning, every dark-liveried coachman he sees in London terrifies him, compels him to speed up; his sense of being followed increases. There are three days left before Mohammad is condemned. He cases the next house in the afternoon and plans to enter that very night. But nerves begin to overwhelm him as he stands above the chimney. The fear inside him now seems greater than the rage. He is losing the smoldering energy needed to attempt these dangerous break-ins. The reality of it all is setting in.

But down the chimney he goes.

He need not have worried. Searching this house turns out to be easier than the first. When he arrives, the interior is so dark that he can't locate his emergency exit. Trying not to panic, imagining how impossible it will be to find the evidence he needs when essentially blind, he goes down on all fours and finds his way through the ground floor to the front door. There: that's his way out.

Once he is near it, he can see a little better: the moon shines brightly through a window in the stone-floored entrance hall. Just as he turns to move up the stairs and search the house, something catches his eye. Leaning against the wall beside the umbrella stand are two crutches. They are long and thick and obviously belong to a man: the owner of the house.

Sherlock hadn't observed the gentleman outside his home that morning. During the short stretch the boy took to survey the house, the master hadn't made a single appearance.

A pair of crutches? What could that mean? The man has either suffered a recent injury, or . . . Sherlock decides to look around. At first he doesn't find what he is searching for, but after a few silent footfalls back into the dining room, he sees it: a photograph. It sits on the mantle over the fireplace. He takes it back to the entrance and examines it in the glow of the moon. There are five people in the picture: a woman, three children, and a gentleman . . . on crutches. Sherlock squints and looks down at the man's feet. He has wooden legs.

It is elementary. This war veteran isn't his villain, either. He can't have been the man who brutally murdered a healthy young woman strong enough to gouge out a man's eye; he can't have been the man who ran from the scene and leapt into that black coach with the red fittings.

Sherlock can go. But he doesn't want to climb back up the chimney, doesn't have the heart now. He is feeling overwrought and simply wants out.

And so he makes a careless decision. He retraces his steps to the door, unlocks it from the inside, and walks out the front steps onto the street.

He can't bolt the door again from the outside. So he leaves it unlocked.

The next day, slithering through the narrow arteries of Soho, Sherlock hears something on wide Regent Street that almost makes him faint. It is the cry of a child, a young girl. He can hear her shouting above all other sounds in the din: "ARAB WILL SWING!"

She is repeating it at the top of her lungs. When he draws closer he can see her standing there in her soiled dress, about Irene's age but much smaller, with straggly black hair and a dark complexion, deformed in size. She holds a clutch of the latest edition of the *Daily News*.

Across Regent Street, a skinny boy is competing with her, yelling so loudly that Sherlock can hear his every word. "PENNY ILLUSTRATED!" he cries, surveying the crowds, anxious for a sale. "ADALJI'S TRIAL IN TWO DAYS!" He holds his sheets high in the air. "DEATH SHALL SURELY FOLLOW!"

Sherlock can feel the blood drain from his face. Seeing this in black and white makes it horribly real. And the paper's assurance of an immediate execution shoots another terror into his mind: if they hang Mohammad . . . what would they do to *him*, the accomplice? His pulse starts to race. They are *all* running out of time.

He has just two days and two houses. The murderer *has* to be in one of them. But at the very time when he needs to move faster, is he in an impossible situation? He thinks of what happened last night. Did he leave a trail behind . . . footprints? Has he aroused suspicion? Will someone be waiting for him the next time he goes to Mayfair, a runaway coach or a long-bladed knife poised to take his life? And what are the chances he will be as lucky in the last two houses as he's been in the first? In them, almost as if invisible powers were guiding him, he had found what he'd been looking for without putting himself in peril. His mother believes in ghosts – she loves séances where people sit at tables and call on the spirits of the dead. Rose would say that a ghost had been leading him. But will a friendly phantom guide him again?

There is only one way to find out.

Fear almost consumes him as he readies himself that night. He has to force himself back to Mayfair. His whole body is shaking as he finds the street that runs almost all the way through the neighborhood near fashionable Park Lane.

The last two houses on his list are on the same avenue, about a dozen residences apart and on either side. So far, he'd started at the top of his mother's note and simply moved down. Tonight, he's decided to play the odds in his deadly game of housebreaking roulette – he's picked the fourth home.

A large residence at the corner of the street has a wooden drainage pipe running up its side. He decides to climb it, placing his feet on the iron rings that hold it to the wall. On this roof, Sherlock will be only five dwellings from his target. But just as he reaches his arm up the pipe and puts his left foot onto a ring, he glimpses something moving on the street. Someone is walking past. He or she seems to be taking forever. Flattened against the building, thankful to be dressed as a chimney sweep with his face blackened, he peeks out.

It's Rose Holmes!

She is walking as if the weight of Westminster Abbey were on her shoulders and as if the flat street were steeper than old Ludgate Hill. Her face is cast down and she holds a piece of paper in one hand.

Sherlock rushes out to her. As he approaches she gasps. The look of fear on her face pains him.

"Mother, it's me," he says under his breath.

"Sherlock?"

He pulls her back from the gaslight into a shadow.

"What clothes are you . . . ?" she asks, then stops. "Oh, yes," she nods, putting it all together.

"I'm getting closer," says Sherlock.

"Thank God." She crosses herself in the manner of her high-church Anglican ancestors, something he has rarely seen her do.

"Mother, it's past midnight!"

"Yes." She seems resigned to something.

"But why are you still . . . "

"It was a very long day, son. There were five daughters in the last home where I taught. The lady is having a birthday celebration tomorrow for her two-year-old son. They all had to memorize songs. I finished just a few hours ago and then I sat outside looking at the sky."

He hopes that explains her lethargy. There's no beer on her breath, but her mind doesn't seem fully engaged. Something is distracting her.

"What is this?" He motions to the piece of paper.

"Oh . . . nothing, really."

She puts it into a pocket in her dress.

"Nothing?"

What is she hiding? She is never good at keeping secrets from him.

"I have a job tomorrow. This is the address," she admits. "The offer came at the last minute – a message delivered by coach to the house. Word of good help spreads quickly around here." She smiles weakly. "The gentleman wants me to tutor at his house tomorrow." She swallows as if there is a lump in her throat. Then she shakes her head and her voice sounds stronger. "I must get home."

"Be careful," says her son, barely listening because his thoughts are fixed on her sadness.

"Sherlock, I know how to keep safe on the streets. You know that."

She reaches up and gently brushes the back of her right hand across his cheek down to his chin, and smiles at him. Then she leaves without saying good-bye. She doesn't need to – that caress always means farewell, every night as she sits on his bed before he goes to sleep.

He watches her walk away. He has a bad feeling. He should have insisted on looking at the paper.

Moments later he is on the roof of the house, moving silently along in the dark London sky. It is cool tonight and feels as if it's going to rain again. He has counted the number of homes he has to walk over. But when he is still two away, he hears something that makes him drop to the roof tiles.

It is the baying of a hound.

It sounds close and it sounds big: a deep, evil bark that resounds in the throat of a giant dog and threatens anyone who nears with a grisly fate. It echoes in the night and drifts away.

He slowly rises to his feet and silently moves again, up and down on the steep surfaces.

On the roof of the last house before his target, he has to leap over a little passageway. It isn't far across, perhaps four feet – chances are he'll make it, but he'll have to do it well and land quietly. He lies on his stomach and sticks his head out over the edge, looking straight down. The drop is frightening. If he misses he'll be in pieces on the ground.

Sherlock closes his eyes and says a little prayer. To whom, he isn't sure: to his mother's God, his father's, Mohammad's? *Whoever will listen*, he thinks. *Whoever will care.* When he opens his eyes, still looking straight down, two other eyes are staring back up at him.

They are framed by a massive dark head and sharp teeth. The boy hears a growl.

He rams his head back from the opening. Just his luck – the hound is at the house he intends to enter!

He rolls over on his back and stares up at the black sky. What now? He thinks of the property below him, a little yard at the back, surrounded by a high, black iron fence with spears on top that runs up the passage and around to the front of the house. Huge walnut trees tower above the street, hanging out over the roofs. He looks around. Walnuts – there are still some on the roof from last autumn. He stands, gathers up a few, moves back from the edge of the passageway so he can't be seen, and tosses them gently into the backyard. He hears the hound bound away. Seconds later, he flies through the air and alights as gently as possible on the suspect's roof.

The next few moments are some of the longest in his life. He listens to the hound running for the walnuts, its heavy breathing, its whimpers as it retrieves its prizes, and its scamper back to its spot underneath the roof. He peers over the edge. The dog is looking up, but not at him. It thinks he is still on the other roof. Perfect. So far, it isn't barking.

He waits until he can't wait anymore. No noises come from within the house – they haven't heard any sounds from the roof. The hound's breathing begins to subside, it yawns and sits down, still facing the opposite rooftop.

Sherlock rises and walks up to the chimney as if he were treading on glass. He is getting better at this. Down he goes and emerges into another dark dining room, ground floor. The front door is where it should be. Everything is in place.

But this time, he won't be so lucky. There won't be any little hall tables with glass eyes in little boxes, no crutches or photographs, no obvious proof of the owner's innocence sitting around in the outer rooms for him to observe.

Sherlock slips up the grand marble steps to the first floor. He walks down the hall . . . drawing room on the right, study to the left. The latter is a good place to search . . . but not the best. He can't waste time. He has to find the man's most private room, where he would be most apt to hide things – where he himself would be. Sherlock climbs another flight of stairs like a ghost . . . and enters the master's bedroom.

The door is only slightly ajar so he has to push it open a little more. It moves smoothly. The room is crowded with furniture, dimly evident in the moonlight that has peeked between the clouds and slipped through the slight opening in the drapes – writing desk, washstand, cabinet, chairs and other objects he can't quite distinguish. Another doorway leads to a dressing room. And there, across the room in a big bed with carved posts . . . is the sound of someone sleeping.

His feet are glued to the floor, their muscles held so tense they won't function. He takes a silent breath, a deep one, and makes himself move in a crouch. Where should he search? What should he search for? First he'll try the desk. Maybe there is something there, something the villain might hide from his wife . . . a letter?

Then he makes a terrible decision. He decides to move quickly to the desk to get this over with. He takes a long stride and stumbles over something – a footstool. He lands on the floor . . . and rolls under the washstand.

"What?" says a slurred voice.

He can't believe it. It's a woman. There is movement in the bed. A body moving and then . . . another!

He is sure this is the master's bedroom . . . but there are two people in the bed.

Sherlock lies under the washstand until his legs feel stiff. There are no more stirrings. Finally, he slides out. He doesn't care about the desk anymore. He crawls over to the bed and raises his head until his eyes peek up over its foot.

Two people lie there asleep. But he can't make out anything about them.

He stands up. Sherlock Holmes stands to his full height – and still can't tell. So . . . he creeps around to the side of the bed and looks down. He is standing right over the two sleeping bodies. His heart is racing.

It's the gentleman and his wife . . . wrapped in each other arms.

Quivering and anxious to leave, he wants this to be proof of the man's innocence. It seems impossible that this loving husband can be the villain. He wants to go *now*. Get out of this bedroom and out of this house. But as he turns he notices that *he is being watched!* In the dim moonlight, a human eye is floating in a gleaming glass of water and staring into his face. He starts and his leg touches the little table near the bed where the glass sits. The whole thing tilts and the eyeball rolls, tinkling against the glass. In the bed, both bodies stir.

Sherlock turns and flees the bedroom, moving so fast that it's difficult to keep his footsteps quiet. Outside the doorway, he lurches to his left, rushes down the hall, and soon finds the top of the stairs. He takes a much wider turn than he should.

His foot catches something, the leg of a piece of furniture.

He stumbles and falls, crashing to the floor, the fancy cabinet almost landing on top of him.

He springs to his feet and flies down the stairs like a swallow. Violins are playing in his head.

The way out!

He hears a man shout from the bedroom. The whole house awakening, servants hitting the floors upstairs. The master's feet pound into the hallway and rush to the top of the steps.

The front door!

Swooping off the bottom steps, Sherlock makes for it. He drives the heavy bolt back and heaves.

It won't open.

The gentleman is thudding down the staircase,

shouting amid the sound of other voices, and of something wooden and steel being pulled from a wall.

A rifle!

Sherlock feels for another bolt on the door, there it is . . . and another. He drives them both back, yanks the door open, and whacks it closed behind him.

Then a sudden realization hits him like a punch.

The hound! He has forgotten about the hound.

He hears it instantly, bounding around from the passageway, so large when he sees it up close that its massive head seems as high as his shoulder, some sort of evil hybrid dog the size of which he could never have imagined, capable of seizing him by the throat and tearing it out in one rip.

Sherlock looks toward the wrought-iron fence. It is as high as his head and pointed at the tips like spears from the Dark Continent.

He has no choice. He heads for it.

The hound's hot breath is at his back.

He reaches the fence and leaps as high as he can. One hand seizes the horizontal bar at the top, the other the sharp tip of a spearhead. He can feel it go into his flesh, touching the bone. Sending his scream and pain deep into himself, he jerks the wounded hand off the spear and onto the horizontal bar and pulls himself up.

But the hound can leap too. It sails through the air as he snaps his feet up to the top of the fence, pulled by the strength of his arms. One leg goes over the spears, out toward the street.

The hound catches the other.

Its teeth enter his calf, tearing into the flesh. But when the giant canine opens its mouth again to strengthen its grip, to crunch bone . . . the boy is gone. He whips his wounded leg over the fence and lands, almost on his face.

Sherlock runs, ignoring the pain in his hand and leg. He puts his head back, chest out, pumps the air with his arms, and dashes down the stately street out into the rest of London, and on and on until he is sure no one is following and he is deep in the city, in The Seven Dials, down another dark alleyway. He collapses in a heap against a wall and squirms into a dustman's mound of stinking rubbish and refuse. Buried under it, his chest heaving so hard that the mound looks alive, Sherlock isn't thinking about his wounds. His mind is back in that bedroom.

They were wrapped in each other's arms.

And there's something else.

He hadn't been able to make out the color of the iris on the false eye when he first saw it submerged in the water, but he'd noticed something else when it rolled. It had no initials. Mr. Lear's do. That eyeball *must* have come from a different manufacturer than the murderer's.

The gentleman in that second-last house is not his villain.

Whether Sherlock falls asleep or blacks out he doesn't know, but within minutes his consciousness is gone.

"One left," he murmurs, just before he fades away.

21

DEATH

He wakes in the morning with a searing pain in his leg. There were special physicians who tended to his mother's family – he wishes he could go to one now. His father has told him about infection and that possibility worries him. It can kill. He pulls up his trouser leg and looks at the ugly wound, caked with blood. A message courses through his brain. *Survive.* Before long, he thinks of something that might help.

It starts to rain. He sets off through the streets, eastbound, aware that a noose is tightening around his neck: the injury may be growing worse and Mayfair is surely going on alert.

But he has to go back there, tonight. All he can hope is that the gentleman in that last house didn't see him clearly and can't tell the police that a tall, thin boy with dark hair, dressed like a chimney sweep, was in his very bedroom.

At Fetter Lane he notices that someone has dropped a newspaper against a red pillar box on a dirty footpath. He snatches it up and reads as he walks.

Crime pages.
Here it is . . .

Mayfair last night . . . break-in reported . . . owner
could not see the perpetrator in the darkness of
his house.

Sherlock looks up to the sky for an instant, thankful. He
reads on.

The police are concerned about goings-on in
Mayfair . . . a door was reported to have been
unlocked from the inside the night before . . .

So, that's the way it will be – he will have to enter that
last house with a Bobbie on every Mayfair corner. The solution to the crime is within his grasp, but will his pursuers
let him solve it?

He is sure that some of the bottles and flasks he noticed
in the chemical laboratory at St. Bartholomew's Hospital
contain disinfectant, the new way of killing infection that
his father has often spoken of – Wilber read about micro-
scopic bacteria in the writings of the great French scientist
Louis Pasteur, and scoffed at the idea that bad smells infected
people and that fly maggots should be used to eat dying

flesh and save only parts of infected limbs. Science, Wilber knew, could do better.

Sherlock sneaks into St. Bart's again, entering by the same arched back door. He knows where to find the lab and what he is looking for inside. But someone is there when he arrives, likely a medical student. He waits until the white-coated, thick-set, young man leaves. He slips in. It takes a long time to find what he needs, and his fear grows as the clock on the wall ticks. He searches label after label. Finally, he spots a small bottle containing a clear liquid identified as "Lister's Carbolic Acid Solution," drops it into a pocket, and makes off down the white corridors, passing the man in the white coat. He hobbles away as fast as he can, and when he gets to the streets, keeps moving. On an embankment down by the Thames he raises his bloodied pant leg and pours the potent elixir over the wound.

He cries out. He has to. The pain is unlike anything he has ever felt before, like someone is burning his flesh with a firebrand. His shriek goes out across the Thames and is swallowed up. The liquid bubbles on the injury, beginning to destroy the infection. He drops more onto his skewered hand.

Across the Thames . . . that's where he wants to go before he returns to Mayfair . . . because he is faltering. It seems like suicide to attempt this last break-in, the odds are so highly stacked against him. Should he go home? Just briefly?

He needs to see Rose. What he hopes to gain, he isn't sure. Perhaps she will convince him not to go. And that

would be a godsend. Or maybe she will give him the courage
to do it? He wonders if he wants that.

Perhaps he just wants to see her for the last time.

The sky clears as he heads south.

It is amazing how easy it has become for him to enter
a house unseen. Malefactor would be impressed. Sitting
alone in their flat, which seems even smaller and more piti-
able now that he has been inside the mansions of Mayfair,
Sherlock realizes that he won't see his father tonight. It's a
Friday – the day when Wilber stays late to clean the doves'
cages. What a job for a man once destined to be a professor
of natural philosophy at the University College of London.

There are many injustices in the world, thinks the
boy. But some are worse than others. You can hate someone
because he's poor, because of the clothes he wears, or for his
political views. But a person can change that. If you hate
someone for being a Jew or an Arab, he cannot rub off his
skin. That sort of prejudice is the greatest injustice . . . next
to taking someone's life.

It has to be about six o'clock, he guesses. Rose should
be here soon.

The sun glows into the flat, warming his face, bringing a slight smile to his lips.

He doesn't bother to read his father's books or drink
from one of his mother's two chipped teacups set on the
shelf above the fireplace. He just stares out the little back

window where he saw the crows gather, waiting for her. As the sun starts to set, everything begins to darken.

So does his mood.

Something isn't right. Time passes. Why would she be so late two nights in a row?

The room grows darker. He lights a candle. Where is she? Fear begins to grow inside him, spreading out from his stomach like a fire.

Where is she?

He gets up and paces, walking as silently as he can, disguised as a chimney sweep in his own home. It has become completely black outside.

There is a rustling at the door. Finally!

What if it isn't her? He doesn't care anymore. He rushes to the door and flings it open.

Again, he sees a look of terror in his mother's face. Reaching out with both arms, he pulls her indoors and wraps her in his arms. But something isn't right. She feels weak in his embrace, though her heart is racing.

"Are you all right, mother?"

"I'm fine, Sherlock. They kept me late. I must sit down."

She staggers across the room and falls onto the couch. The burning inside him, which had subsided momentarily, rises again.

"It was very strange," she mumbles.

Her speech is slurred, but he doesn't smell ale.

"What was strange, mother?"

"Tea? . . . Do you have some tea you might give me, young man?"

"What was strange!?" he shouts, taking her face into his hands. The pupils in her eyes aren't right. *Oh, God!*

"The gentleman . . . the gentleman of the house . . . "

"Yes?"

"Gave me tea . . . made tea himself . . . and served it to me . . . a strange brew . . . it made me . . . "

Her voice fades. Something falls from her hand: the same piece of paper he saw her carrying last night. He sees the address on it this time. The very house he intends to enter tonight. The house where the villain surely lives!

Rose tries to rally herself. "I didn't want to tell you that it was one of the four houses."

"Mother, the men in the others are *innocent!*"

"I thought I might learn something. . . . I didn't want you to go away. . . . The man gave me an awful smile when he showed me out . . . said Mayfair knows when outsiders ask inappropriate questions . . . that he'd noticed the other burgled houses belonged to his one-eyed friends . . . that he'd been speaking to all the servants . . . "

She collapses in his arms.

"MOTHER!"

As he holds her closely he can barely feel the beat of her heart. Lifting her in his arms, he is alarmed at how light she is . . . like a bird. When he sets her on her bed she is completely limp. Her eyes open briefly.

"You have much to do in life," she says clearly.

Then her eyes close. Frantically he pulls the covers over her and takes her white hand in his. It has no life. He feels her wrist for a pulse.

There is none.

The beautiful, worry-wrinkled eyelids are still. The mouth is slightly open. Her lips are dry and her face flushed red. His father has taught him the properties of nearly every chemical mixture known to man, and their symptoms should they be ingested . . . especially the lethal ones.

Poison! Deadly nightshade!

"MOTHER!" he screams again and presses his forehead to hers. His chest heaves and his lungs fill and empty of air. He stays that way for a long while, holding her, waiting for her breathing to come back. But it won't.

When he finally rises, his face looks like a devil's mask. Hatred is carved into it. He seizes their table and throws it across the room with the strength of a demon. It crashes and splinters against the wall. The sound echoes in the little flat and out into the street.

He races to the window, smashes it through with his fist, and thrusts his head into the outside air.

"JUSTICE!!"

He howls it into the night, his head thrown back, his teeth like fangs, his eyes two glowing black coals. When he opens the door, he nearly rips it from its hinges. He swoops down the stairs.

Someone is coming up toward him.

If it isn't his father, he will kill with his bare hands.

But he doesn't. And it isn't Wilber.

Irene is struggling up the steps.

"Sherlock!"

She has never seen a human being look like this before.

It is as if his face, that dark, handsome young face, is lit from within. The eyes are all black – the gray irises gone.

He pauses for only a second. "Stay away from me!" he warns her.

He shoves her, wounded as she is, and nearly knocks her down the stairs. He doesn't give her another thought. In minutes he is back across the Thames . . . and headed for Mayfair.

He has something to do on the way. Just below London Bridge on the north side, is Mohammad Adalji's butcher shop. The old butcher likely doesn't have a new boy yet. He'll be cleaning the knives himself – just finishing up.

The Tower of London looms to his right but Sherlock doesn't look at it tonight. His hands are clutched in fists, the knuckles white, and he is running, tears pouring down his face. Mohammad told him exactly how to find the shop.

The dim light is on when he arrives.

Sherlock tries the door. It's unlocked. He opens it and deftly slips inside. The butcher has his back to him, cleaning and sharpening the knives. They lie on a thick wooden table, splattered with blood. The boy wipes his face dry.

He doesn't bother hiding his presence. He knows what he wants – he *has* to have it – and he is certain he can outrun the old man.

There are at least a dozen blades to choose from. Every one of them will do the job. The sharpened knives are to the old man's right, the dirty ones to the left. It will be harder to grab a sharp weapon, but Sherlock doesn't care – that's what he needs.

He eyes a big blade, long and serrated, sharp as a barber's razor, not too long to be concealed in his clothing.

The butcher is gripping another knife in his hand. He holds it up to examine it and when he does, he sees a boy behind him, reflected in the gleaming blade. It makes him start. The lad looks like he's climbed up from hell that very evening.

Sherlock lunges forward and seizes the knife. The man gasps and draws back, holding his big blade in front of him. He expects the worst: to be butchered with one of his own tools by this tall child from Hades.

The boy pivots and flees.

By the time the butcher has recovered his senses, by the time he has stepped to the street and screamed "Thief!" into the night, there is no sign of Sherlock Holmes.

He runs toward Mayfair, concentrating on a single thought. It is the hardest thing he's ever had to do: he has to control his rage and his grief. He *absolutely* must to gain this vengeance. He needs to be ice cold, as villainous and as clever as a fox. He thinks of the things his mother has told him about performing.

"When an opera singer creates a character, she collects all the emotions she thinks that person might have . . . buries them deep inside her and then uses them."

He buries his boiling anger, his white-hot rage. He wants it to power, not overwhelm him. He wants to *use* it!

He can't make mistakes, not if he wants his mother's due. Tears come to his eyes again. He stops them, tucks his chin down onto his chest, holds his jaw tight, and glares into the darkness.

He flies across London in the night and lands at the Mayfair address.

The house is across the street from the one he'd been in the previous night. The Peelers are everywhere. He sees half a dozen before he even arrives. On the street where he will operate, there are two: one at each end of the avenue. His house is in the middle.

He darts over an iron fence, into a little backyard, and begins moving behind the houses, up and down like a snake over the separating walls.

Then he comes to the house he wants.

It has a long lane and a little mews and stable at the back. That's unusual. Most stables are kept on smaller nearby streets, so the mansions are far from the smell. But because this house has its own little lane, a small additional stable has been built at the back, perhaps just for vehicles. A high wall runs from it along the backyard to the house. That will help him get onto the roof. Entering via the chimney is still the best idea – no one has figured out how he's gotten into the other houses – he hasn't been recognized. The chimney is still the way.

But just as he is about to scale the wall, he hears a noise behind him. His hand goes to his knife and he drops down behind the wall. Someone is inside the stable!

In seconds the two front doors swing open and a man emerges carrying a lantern. His frame is wide like a rugby player's; and his thick head, like a bulbous canning jar on his shoulders, is shaved to the scalp. Something is familiar about him but from behind the wall, the boy can't see him clearly. The man closes the doors and walks down the lane toward the street, glancing around, going right past the boy, settling a black hat onto his head and a dark scarf around his neck.

Sherlock waits until the footsteps fade.

Now he can get on the roof. But something makes him want to look inside the stable. Those wide, rugby shoulders, that black hat and scarf . . . he's seen them before.

He advances down the lane and pulls open the stable doors.

A dark coach . . . but it is brown. He closes the entrance.

Then he smells something. *Paint.* Someone has recently painted the coach. Sherlock looks down the street in the direction the thick-shouldered man has gone. Rushing to the street, the boy sees him pass under a streetlamp, revealing himself from head to boots . . . wearing a *black-liveried coachman's uniform with red stripes.*

Sherlock reaches for the knife. But then he pauses. Even if he can kill this brute, it won't eliminate the real villain. The coachman had been doing a job, following a meddling boy and girl, scaring them . . . for his living. Sherlock looks at the darkened house. The coachman isn't the source of evil here. His real prey is inside.

Though standing on the wall allows him to start halfway up the house, there are no iron rungs or drainage pipes here. He'll have to climb the outside of the building. It is an ornate home, filled with tall windows and deep frames and covered with green ivy. Up he goes like a spider, from wide windowframe to windowframe, up the ivy between them, silently and stealthily, until he reaches the roof. Nothing will stop him now.

He is down the chimney in minutes. He doesn't even look for an emergency way out. It doesn't matter anymore. He wants two things: real evidence of the villain's guilt . . . and the villain himself.

He sweeps across the dining room and up the stairs to the first floor, then the second. Once he is there, it is obvious where the master sleeps. And that he sleeps alone.

The boy makes his way to the big double doors at the end of the hall.

His mind is racing – the coachman, the freshly painted carriage . . . the poison on his mother's lips. There is no doubt now that *this* is the right place.

Evidence . . . then the villain. He feels for his knife.

The room smells of tobacco – a man's lair.

Sherlock closes the door gently behind him. The almost paralyzing nervousness he felt in the other houses isn't in him tonight. Vengeance is. His rage makes him strong and determined.

He crouches down and cases the room.

The man is snoring in the bed, lying on his back, the outline of his round gut rising and falling. Sherlock turns around. There is a cabinet, a washstand, a wardrobe . . . and a small writing desk.

This is *the* desk. It has to be. The one he has been searching for since he began entering the houses. All the evidence is coming together. He has to cinch it now. Malefactor said that when he found that one piece of evidence, that vital piece . . . everything would be solved.

Sherlock crawls across the carpet to the desk. It feels glossy, as if heavily stained. There are initials carved on the middle drawer. He runs his hands along the letters: J . . . T . . . R.

That's the name – the last one left on his mother's list. The desk belongs to the owner of this house and no one else . . . his own private depository.

Sherlock starts going through the drawers, finding banknotes and leaving them, papers that mean nothing, and photographs that he drops to the floor.

In the bed, the man stirs.

There has to be *something*, somewhere in this desk.

In the last drawer, the one on the left side, Sherlock finds a small box. It is heavy and made of iron. He tries to open it. It won't budge. He holds it up in the moonlight and discovers a thick lock.

Sherlock remembers Malefactor's lecture on picking them.

You need two sharp objects. He has one – a hatpin he found on the street a few days ago. He'd even bent its end, ready for action.

He pulls the knife from his clothing. Its tip is like

a pin: the business end of a butcher's blade that can slice through flesh as if it is butter.

Sherlock has heard Malefactor's lock speech more than once. Fascinated by mathematics in all its forms, the young crime lord talks about the geometry of the interior, its tumblers, how they all need to fall into position for the lock to be sprung. You have to feel it: you have to click one and then the other and then the last.

Sherlock penetrates the lock with the tip of the knife, then slides the hatpin in too. He feels around inside. He begins pushing the tumblers back. *Click.* He can almost hear it. *Click.* There is the second one. *Click.* . . . The last.

Presto! He turns the blade. The lock opens.

He puts the knife and hatpin back into his coat, sets the heavy box on the floor, and lifts the lid.

There is only one object inside.

A purse.

It is embroidered with beads to form exotic birds, and splashed with red, which Sherlock at first thinks is part of the design. But it is raised and crusted on the surface.

Blood!

Some of the beadwork has been torn off.

Fingers trembling, he opens the purse.

Will there by anything in it?

There are a few coins, a small pot of rouge, a handkerchief.

He is about to put it down, when he feels something else inside: a little pouch, like a secret pocket. It is difficult to open. He reaches in and finds a letter.

The killer took this purse in order to make the crime look like a robbery. He kept it here because the police had the Arab in custody and would never come to his Mayfair mansion. He would dispose of it, wisely, after the murder was long forgotten. But Sherlock is betting the villain didn't search the purse thoroughly, had no reason to, and didn't know this letter was hidden inside. If it contains anything incriminating, it will be Lillie's vengeance from the grave.

Sherlock unfolds the sheet. But he can't read it. It is too dark. He walks over to the window, an arm's length from the head of the bed. The man is snoring, his eyelids moving rapidly.

Sherlock reads in the slashes of moonlight.

Lillie,

I implore you to read this carefully. If you do not desist from these evil plans of yours, I shall not be responsible for my actions. I have position and I will protect it, believe me. Blackmail is blackmail, whether perpetrated by a criminal or the belle of the ball. You cannot tell my wife of our affairs, I will not pay you for your silence, and you and I cannot continue together. That is simply our situation. We must go our separate ways. We were meant to enjoy one another, but never more than that. My world is not yours and never shall be.

Yes, I will meet you one more time. Tomorrow. There is a little lane off Old Yard

Street in Whitechapel, west side, absolutely secluded. Be there at the stroke of two in the morning. I won't meet you anywhere else. I know you will come, and I know you are familiar with those streets.

Tell no one of this. Those who interfere with me, do so at their peril.

J.T.R.

Sherlock crams the letter back into the purse. He shoves it all into his pocket.

He looks at the man in the bed. *He hates him.* It is absolute and pure hatred.

And it is time for this beast to die.

Rose Holmes might be nobody, Sherlock and Mohammad might be too, but this villain is going to pay, just as if they were all equals. There will be justice tonight. He will make things right with the violent plunge of his big butcher's blade. He will carve up this man like the pig he has proven himself to be.

The boy reaches into his coat and pulls out the knife. It gleams in the moonlight. He steps up to the edge of the bed and raises it high over his victim. The man is lying on his back. The blade will go straight into the heart. Sherlock imagines the man's gasp.

This is for all the injustice he has suffered; for all the hate everywhere in the world . . . and for Rose Sherrinford Holmes.

Justice!

His eyes are black stars. But something makes him pause.

Something deep inside him, borne of the scientific wisdom of his decent father and the love of his beautiful mother, murmurs that this will *not* be justice. It will be murder. And he, Sherlock Holmes, will be as bad as the man he kills. His mother will have died in vain. Irene will have been wounded for nothing.

Should he do what is right? He glares down at the man. Or wrong? He slowly lowers the blade, and hides it in his clothes.

He has the glass eye, the bracelet, the coachman, the freshly painted carriage, the blood-splattered coin purse, and even the letter. This man will swing. He will pay the price. Sherlock has him.

But he isn't satisfied. He wants one more thing. One thing that will say to anyone, absolutely beyond any doubt, that this is the villain.

He thinks of the eyeball in the dirt in the dog kennel on Montague Street. He thinks of that day, not long ago, when Irene identified its color, its unique brown iris with the violet fleck knifing into it. Only one man has eyes like that.

He turns to the sleeping body. He thinks for a moment and then smiles. He raises his left hand high over his head and brings it down with a resounding *smack* across the sleeping face, slapping the man with every ounce of strength he has.

The head jerks back and the lids snap open in terror. One socket is empty. An eye stares back from the other.

Brown . . . with flecks of violet.

Sherlock leaves the house by the front door. He walks down the stairs and out the main entrance. No one follows him. On the street, he flies away. When the man in the bedroom finally regains his senses, by the time his servants rise and come to him, the boy has vanished into the night.

22

SHERLOCK HOLMES

Inspector Lestrade of Scotland Yard finds a most curious collection of items on his desk the following morning, the day of Mohammad's trial. There is a glittering bracelet, a glass eye splattered with blood, and a stained purse with a letter inside. Delivered to the night sergeant by an errand boy with his cap pulled down over his eyes, it is crudely wrapped in a newspaper. Across the sheet torn from *The Illustrated Police News*, written with the sharp end of something dipped in watered-down soot, is a detailed explanation of what happened on the night of the Whitechapel murder. It answers every question anyone could possibly have, tells of the sacrifice of brave Rose Sherrinford Holmes, and identifies the murderer and where he can be found.

Propped against the stone fence in a deserted Trafalgar Square in the pale and foggy dawn, Sherlock is seeing it now: the entire murder. Swooping down from the black sky, he lands on the edge of the building on Old Yard Street off Whitechapel.

Settling his oily feathers, he turns when he hears her rushing toward him down below, the sound echoing in the street. He cocks his head and trains his sharp eye on the scene. Observe. The beautiful woman, Lillie Irving, is running, her jewelry glowing, anxious to impress someone. *Shining.* It makes him mutter, his dark tongue poised in his beak. She hastens into an alley and turns to wait, her chest heaving, pretty hands nervously clutching a purse. He lifts off and lands above her, cocking his head again. Something else is glowing in the moonlight on the filthy ground not far from her . . . a knife.

A street away a black coach comes to a halt and a large, middle-aged man steps down onto the pavement, the carriage bouncing as his weight leaves it. He is rushing too, and soon has entered the alley. Sherlock's heart beats faster in his black breast.

She reaches out tenderly for the man when he nears. He grabs her wrist and something glittery flies off. Her other arm reaches out. He pushes her back. She begins to cry. Then she grows angry. She is threatening him. He is warning her. She rears and slaps his face and then shoves him. He staggers and steps on something. He picks it up.

Up above, Sherlock cries out as he sees what it is. . . . *Mohammad's blade.*

Down it comes. Once. She screams. A pretty white hand comes up like a cat's paw, nails out, and grips the man's face, a finger digging into the eye, gouging. He screams. The knife comes up in the moonlight again.

Twice.

Three times.

Four.

Five.

She falls, gasps, and is still.

The man looks skyward for a second. A crow gazes back. It's *him* – the man in the bed in Mayfair!

The murderer looks down at the knife. Drops it. Hesitates. Snatches up the purse. Runs. Around the corner, holding his face, making for the coach. He enters it on the fly, shouting something to his black-liveried coachman, and they race away at full speed.

The murder done, the crow drops down. Time to search for those shiny things.

Sherlock can see them in the dawn. As always, they are gathered on Morley's Hotel and atop palatial Northumberland House, on its golden lion across the square. They are watching, preening their black feathers, sticking close to each other, their brains alert. The boy smiles weakly.

He doesn't leave the square all day. He can't move. A few people begin to appear and then a few more. Then things start to bustle. Malefactor materializes before long, and eyes him from a distance through the crowd, not sure why he is leaving himself so visible to the police.

But the Bobbies already have their man – an hour before, a whole flock of the Force arrested the killer in his Mayfair mansion, Lestrade at their head, his chest puffed out.

Sherlock stares back at Malefactor. The criminal can see that there is no more fear in the half-breed boy's cloudy gray eyes. Something has changed. Forever.

Malefactor nods at Holmes, signals to his swarm, and melts into the crowd.

Over on Bow Street, Mohammad Adalji is stepping out into the sunlight. The fog has lifted; spring is finally here to stay. There is a smile on his face, but wariness remains in his eyes. There have been no explanations, no apologies. He's just been released without comment. Had he been a betting man, he would have wagered that the tall, thin boy with the desperate eyes had something to do with this. *Freedom.* Mohammad walks slowly down Bow Street, but starts to run when he turns at the Strand. He wonders if he should just keep on running. East. East. East. Until he is all the way home.

Sherlock thinks of many things: of his father and wonders what is next; of Irene and wishes he could be with her; and of his mother. But when he thinks of her, he cries. That will not do.

In Southwark, Wilber Holmes is still sitting on the bed in their flat, rocking his wife in his arms. He had come home in the dark and found her there. Hatred changed his life, but couldn't destroy it as long as he had Rose, his beautiful Rose, who had sacrificed her dreams for him. Now she is gone.

Sherlock wipes his eyes and gets ready for the evening papers.

His friend Dupin, the cripple, will find him one. He won't have to wait.

When Big Ben strikes 5:00, the boy makes his way across the square. Dupin sees him coming and looks the other way so the lad can take the freshest edition he's ever held in his hands. The shadows envelop him as he moves into an alcove against a building. The stone surface is cool and clammy.

It is time for a brief moment in the sun amidst the darkness and horror. He gave Lestrade all the details and surely the inspector has told the press: London will at least know that Rose Sherrinford was the bravest and best woman on earth, that she marched into the lair of the murderer, that she loved her son with her life, and that he, Sherlock Holmes, solved the unsolvable crime of the Whitechapel murder. He gave precious freedom to a wrongly accused man, and allowed Lillie Irving to rest in peace. His mother will not have died in vain. She, and he, will at least and at last be . . . somebody.

It is splashed across the front page.

"BRILLIANT MURDER SOLUTION!"

He reads every word. Not one of them is *Holmes*.

There, amongst the many pages of coverage, are illustrations of the triumphant Inspector Lestrade along with his thoughts on his own clever solution to the crime. He holds up the bracelet, the purse, the glass eye, and the letter. The Force, he tells the reporters, doubted that Mr. Adalji was the real villain from the start – they had been watching Mayfair for weeks.

The tall, thin boy's first reaction is despair. He has been fighting to control himself. Now he almost faints, dropping to the ground and pulling his legs up to his chest. Not only has his involvement in this horror killed his mother, but he has buried her deeper in anonymity than she ever was in life.

But then an image of Rose comes to his mind, speaking to him the last time he saw her. He can't collapse. He sits up cross-legged, his big head against the wall. Anger begins to spread through him. He and his mother *will* get their due. He will seek vengeance for *all* who are wronged.

The crows lift off into the dark sky, making their horrible sound. He watches them fly.

What did she say to him just before she died?

"You have much to do in life."

She is right. He knows now what his big brain can accomplish. He has solved a crime that eluded Scotland Yard. Fear had tried to invade him on those rooftops and passions had sometimes made him careless and easier for the police to spot, but he had steeled himself to his task by setting aside his emotions, becoming ice cold, turning himself into a machine. It had proved the right approach. Now, he needs to go further.

He will never allow himself to be emotionally attached to anyone again. Attachments are unaffordable. Instead, he will spend every waking hour seeking justice, as villainous in his search as any criminal. He will become a deadly, thinking force.

They will all pay. He will make them.

No one will ever know the depth of his pain, but those who stand in the way of justice will feel it. He will hide his past and create a new future. Someday everyone will know the name Sherlock Holmes.

The Master looks out at London. The fog is settling. Darkness is falling. He stands up to his full height, shoulders back, and walks into the streets. His gray eyes observe every stimuli, his beak-like nose smells every scent. He doesn't know where he will go or stay, but he knows exactly what he will do.

ACKNOWLEDGMENTS

There were many struggles endured during the writing of this book, but certain extraordinary people made its publication possible because they believed in it and in me. First among these was the publisher of Tundra Books, Kathy Lowinger, whose integrity and courage were (and are) exactly what this project needed; and my fearless agent and friend Pamela Paul who stood by me and this idea during some dark hours. Thanks to both of you for giving me the opportunity to attempt to say something of value with my work.

There are also many folks in my new family at Tundra to thank. Editor extraordinaire Kathryn Cole was an essential companion as we together investigated the mysteries of this story (and my writing); in the end, she was always there with a solution. Catherine Mitchell, Alison Morgan, and Pamela Osti brought their inventive ideas to the concept as well.

And monstrous thanks, of course, to the one and only Sir Arthur Conan Doyle, a moral knight of the 19th century, who loved and hated his fabulous, justice-seeking creation, but gave him to the world, and happily for me, made him unusual, addicted to attention, and oh-so secretive about his past – I hope I have served you and the Master well.

Finally, to my wife Sophie, our three little irregular detectives, and the wonder-dog, Watson, thanks for being my companions in the down-and-up mystery of life.

BE SURE TO READ THE NEXT
FIVE BOOKS IN THIS
AWARD-WINNING SERIES

DEATH IN THE AIR

till reeling from his mother's death, brought about by his involvement in solving London's brutal East End murder, young Sherlock Holmes commits himself to fighting crime . . . and is soon immersed in another case.

While visiting his father at work, Sherlock stops to watch a dangerous high-trapeze performance, framed by the magnificent glass ceiling of the legendary Crystal Palace. But without warning, the aerialist drops, screaming and flailing to the floor. He lands with a sickening thud, just feet away and rolls almost onto the boy's boots. He is bleeding profusely and his body is grotesquely twisted. Leaning over, Sherlock brings his ear up close. "Silence me . . ." the man gasps and then lies still. In the mayhem that follows, the boy notices something amiss that no one else sees – and he knows that foul play is afoot. What he doesn't know is that his discovery will set him on a trail that leads to an entire gang of notorious and utterly ruthless criminals.

VANISHING GIRL

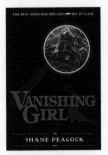

When a wealthy young socialite mysteriously vanishes in Hyde Park, young Sherlock Holmes is compelled to prove himself once more. There is much at stake: the kidnap victim, an innocent child's survival, the fragile relationship between himself and the beautiful Irene Doyle. Sherlock must act quickly if he is to avoid the growing menace of his enemy, Malefactor, and further humiliation at the hands of Scotland Yard.

As twisted and dangerous as the backstreets of Victorian London, this third case in The Boy Sherlock Holmes series takes the youth on a heart-stopping race against time to the countryside, the coast, and into the haunted lair of exotic – and deadly – night creatures.

Despite the cold, the loneliness, the danger, and the memories of his shattered family, one thought keeps Sherlock going; soon, very soon, the world will come to know him as the master detective of all time.

THE SECRET FIEND

In 1868, Benjamin Disraeli becomes England's first
Jewish-born prime minister. Sherlock Holmes wel-
comes the event – but others fear it. The upper classes
worry that the black-haired Hebrew cannot be good
for the empire. The wealthy hear rumblings as the poor
hunger for sweeping improvements to their lot in life. The
winds of change are blowing.

Late one night, Sherlock's admirer and former schoolmate, Beatrice, arrives at his door, terrified. She claims a
maniacal, bat-like man has leapt upon her and her friend on
Westminster Bridge. The fiend she describes is the Spring
Heeled Jack, a fictional character from the old Penny
Dreadful thrillers. Moreover, Beatrice declares the Jack has
made off with her friend. She begs Holmes to help, but he
finds the story incredible. Reluctant to return to detective
work, he pays little heed – until the attacks increase, and
Spring Heeled Jacks seem to be everywhere. Now, all of
London has more to worry about than politics. Before he
knows it, the unwilling boy detective is thrust, once more,
into the heart of a deadly mystery, in which everyone, even
his closest friend and mentor, is suspect.

THE DRAGON TURN

Sherlock Holmes and Irene Doyle are as riveted as the rest of the audience. They are celebrating Irene's sixteenth birthday at The Egyptian Hall as Alistair Hemsworth produces a real and very deadly dragon before their eyes. This single, fantastic illusion elevates the previously unheralded magician to star status, making him the talk of London. He even outshines the Wizard of Nottingham, his rival on and off the stage.

Sherlock and Irene rush backstage after the show to meet the great man, only to witness Inspector Lestrade and his son arrest the performer. It seems one-upmanship has not been as satisfying to Hemsworth as the notion of murder. The Wizard is missing; his spectacles and chunks of flesh have been discovered in pools of blood in Hemsworth's secret workshop. That, plus the fact that Nottingham has stolen Hemsworth's wife away, speak of foul play *and* motive. There is no body, but there has certainly been a grisly death.

In this spine-tingling case, lust for fame and thirst for blood draw Sherlock Holmes one giant step closer to his destiny – master detective of all time.

BECOMING HOLMES

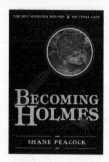

It is the summer of 1870 in London, and death seems to be everywhere; at least it feels that way to Sherlock Holmes. Almost seventeen now, he cannot shake the blackness that has descended upon him. And somewhere in the darkness, Sherlock's great enemy, the villainous Malefactor, is spinning his web of evil, planning who knows what.

Only one thing can rouse the young detective from the depths of despair: the possibility of justice. Holmes uncovers a new and terrible plot unleashed by his nemesis. Prepared to do anything to stop Malefactor, Sherlock sets out to destroy his rival, bringing him and his henchmen down, once and for all. Everything in the brilliant boy's life changes as death knocks again. . . . In this shocking and spine-tingling conclusion to the award-winning series, Sherlock Holmes transforms, becoming the immortal master of criminal detection.

If you enjoyed The Boy Sherlock Holmes Series,
you won't want to miss the first book in
Shane Peacock's thrilling new gothic trilogy,

THE DARK MISSIONS OF
EDGAR BRIM